"Displays Of Machismo Don't Impress Me, Mr. Bennett,"

Kendra said coolly.

"Kendra, I'm trying to do the decent thing, but you're really pushing me."

"Well, excuse me!" She crossed her arms over her breasts. "Since when is discussing my sex life, my experience or lack of same the decent thing to do? What it is, is nosy. You'll fit into this town well, Joseph. You have just the right personality for it."

"Oh, you're asking for it," he said, narrowing his eyes.

"What's next? You put on your sunglasses and do your Italian hit man routine?"

"Will you shut up and listen to me? Believe me, Kendra Smith, I'm very aware that you're a woman. But might I point out that I'm a man?"

Dear Reader:

Series and Spin-offs! Connecting characters and intriguing interconnections to make your head whirl.

In Joan Hohl's successful trilogy for Silhouette Desire— *Texas Gold* (7/86), *California Copper* (10/86), *Nevada Silver* (1/87)—Joan created a cast of characters that just wouldn't quit. You figure out how *Lady Ice* (5/87) connects. And in August, "J.B." demanded his own story—*One Tough Hombre*. In *Falcon's Flight*, coming in November, you'll learn *all* about . . .?

Annette Broadrick's *Return to Yesterday* (6/87) introduced Adam St. Clair. This August *Adam's Story* tells about the woman who saves his life—and teaches him a thing or two about love!

The six Branigan brothers appeared in Leslie Davis Guccione's *Bittersweet Harvest* (10/86) and *Still Waters* (5/87). September brings *Something in Common*, where the eldest of the strapping Irishmen finds love in unexpected places.

Midnight Rambler by Linda Barlow is in October—a special Halloween surprise, and totally unconnected to anything.

Keep an eye out for other Silhouette Desire favorites— Diana Palmer, Dixie Browning, Ann Major and Elizabeth Lowell, to name a few. You never know when secondary characters will insist on their own story. . . .

All the best,

Isabel Swift
Senior Editor & Editorial Coordinator
Silhouette Books

ROBIN ELLIOTT
Lost and Found

Silhouette Desire

Published by Silhouette Books New York

America's Publisher of Contemporary Romance

SILHOUETTE BOOKS
300 East 42nd St., New York, N.Y. 10017

Copyright © 1987 by Joan Elliott Pickart

ISBN: 0-373-05384-3

First Silhouette Books printing October 1987

America's Publisher of Contemporary Romance

Printed in the U.S.A.

Books by Robin Elliott

Silhouette Desire

Call It Love #213
To Have It All #237
Picture of Love #261
Pennies in the Fountain #275
Dawn's Gift #303
Brooke's Chance #323
Betting Man #344
Silver Sands #362
Lost and Found #384

Silhouette Intimate Moments

Gauntlet Run #206

ROBIN ELLIOTT

enjoys reading, knitting and watching football, in addition to writing romance novels. She is the mother of three daughters and the devoted servant of a cocker spaniel named Cricket. Robin also writes under her own name, Joan Elliott Pickart.

For my daughter, Tracey
All grown up and doing fine

One

And then the rabbit ate the geraniums.

It was the last straw, the capper, the event that pushed Kendra Smith's temper to the boiling point. The week had been a study in frustration; she'd had a flat tire matched by a flat spare, an umbrella that had divided into three pieces in the middle of a rainstorm and her first cavity, which resulted in a terror-filled hour in the office of a dentist who seemed to have an unnatural love for garlic. She'd ruined four pairs of panty hose, chipped a fingernail and lost her favorite lipstick.

None of these was a major catastrophe taken individually, but they added up to enough to thoroughly jangle her nerves.

And then the rabbit ate the geraniums.

Kendra stood in her tiny greenhouse and watched in wide-eyed horror as the last of the beautiful red blossoms disappeared into the mouth of the enormous white rabbit. Kendra was momentarily mesmerized by the fascinating motions of the rabbit's lazy chewing combined with the rapid wiggling of its nose. Then, to her utter amazement, she realized that the entire procedure was accompanied by the tinkling of a bell that hung from a blue collar around the rabbit's neck.

"Don't be ridiculous," Kendra muttered, pressing her hand to her forehead. Rabbits didn't wear cute little collars. What was next? Was it going to pull out a watch and announce it was late for a very important date? Oh, Lord, she was cracking up. "Shoo," she said, waving her hands at the animal. "Go away. Shoo."

As if in no particular hurry, the rabbit hopped toward, then around her and went out the door. Kendra spun on her heel and followed it. Across the small yard they went, Kendra feeling more and more like Alice in Wonderland. The rabbit stopped at the wooden fence between her cabin and the one next door, then turned, as though making certain Kendra was still in attendance.

"I'm coming," she said, then silently called herself a complete idiot.

Seemingly satisfied, the rabbit wiggled its nose, then squeezed behind a loose plank in the fence. Kendra dropped to her knees in the damp, cool grass and peered through the narrow opening. The rabbit hopped to the back door of the cabin, then sat up on its hind legs.

"If it rings the doorbell, I'm having myself committed," Kendra muttered. "Besides, that cabin is empty."

Kendra gasped as the screen door of the cabin suddenly opened. Her eyes widened as a man stepped out, then knelt down in front of the rabbit and scratched it behind the ears.

He was a big man—big and dark, and handsome as all get-out. His face was tanned and his hair black and appealingly unruly. His dark eyebrows, straight nose and square chin were unquestionably attractive, and he had a marvelous smile, one that grew larger by the minute and showed pearly white teeth.

His chest, Kendra decided, was a superior example of a bare male chest; tanned, broad and muscular, it was covered with black curls. The hand petting the rabbit's ears had long fingers and a gentle touch, verified by the fact that the rabbit had closed its eyes and seemed to be smiling.

Rabbits didn't smile, Kendra told herself. But then again, who knows what anyone might do when being caressed by that hand. Who was this guy in the cutoff jeans, jeans that displayed powerful legs covered in a dusting of dark hair? That cabin had been empty yesterday. Was he a bum who'd broken in searching for a place to sleep? He didn't look like a bum. Not that she'd ever actually met any bums....

"So, where have you been off to, Homer?" the man said to the rabbit.

Homer? Kendra repeated to herself. What a dumb name for a rabbit. That had been an exceptionally deep, rich voice asking Homer about his morning activities, but it was a dumb name. This man, this hunk, this blatantly sexy male, had a pet rabbit named Homer, a rabbit who wore a blue collar and a bell. Absurd. But whatever Mr. Epitome of Masculinity's choice of pets was, it did not erase the fact that Homer had eaten her geraniums!

As Kendra watched, the man stood up, opened the door, then stepped back for Homer to enter. The man followed the rabbit inside and disappeared from view.

Kendra got to her feet and shook her head. No, she hadn't dreamed the whole thing, she realized. She was awake. Her geraniums had been that rotten rabbit's breakfast. She wanted justice, retribution, compensation for the untimely demise of her beautiful flowers, and once she figured out how best to approach this devastatingly handsome mystery man, she was going to get it.

She stomped across the backyard and entered her cabin, welcoming its warmth after the crisp late-October air. The breeze blowing off the lake held a hint of the colder Michigan weather to come, and Kendra shivered.

How Mr. Body Beautiful could stand traipsing around in nothing more than cutoffs, she didn't know. She also didn't know who he was or why he was all of a sudden in that cabin. Was it smart to go pounding on his door? she wondered. He could be an escaped convict. With a pet rabbit? No, probably not.

Kendra leaned against the counter in her small yellow-and-white kitchen and tapped her finger against her chin. Her blue eyes were narrowed in concentration and her full lips pursed. Her shoulder-length, blond wavy hair was in wild disarray from the brisk breeze off the lake. A baggy sweatshirt concealed the fullness of her breasts beneath, but faded jeans hugged long, slender legs and gently sloping hips.

She'd go calling on her neighbor, Kendra decided. There was no excuse for Homer's criminal behavior. None. Mr. Tantalizing Torso was responsible for his weird pet's actions. However, since he could be a raving lunatic for all she knew, she would arm herself accordingly. Stupid she was not.

With a decisive nod, Kendra left the kitchen and crossed the living room. Her tennis shoes squeaked on the highly polished floor as she went down the hall and into a small bedroom. The spare room contained a twin bed, dresser and junk. It held boxes of this and that, all the things Kendra hadn't had room for when she'd moved to the cabin. She rummaged through the disorganized treasures and found what she was seeking.

A baseball bat.

With a toss of her head, Kendra slung the bat over her shoulder and marched out the front door to the neighboring cabin. Her gaze swept over a silver BMW parked in the driveway, erasing the lingering thought that Mr. Macho Muscles was a bum. She went up the two steps and across the porch, then rapped briskly on the front door.

If the rabbit answered, she decided, she was going to have herself shipped to the funny farm and forget the damn geraniums.

Homer didn't answer the door.

Mr. Sensuous Smile did, and Kendra's mouth dropped open.

He was taller than she'd realized, taller, and broader across his bare shoulders. He was also more deeply tanned and even better-looking than he'd seemed to be when viewed from her peephole through the fence. The man was incredible.

"Well, hello," he said in a rumbly voice, his smile widening from a forty-watt to a hundred-watt dazzler. "What can I do for you? Are you selling baseball bats door-to-door?"

"What?" Kendra asked, momentarily confused. "Oh!" she added, snapping out of her trance. "No. I'm here to . . . to register a complaint against your rabbit."

"I see," he said solemnly, but Kendra was sure, absolutely positive, there was amusement dancing in his dark eyes. "Then perhaps you should come in."

"No, thank you," she said, lifting her chin. "That won't be necessary. I simply wish to inform you that Homer ate six geraniums. Red geraniums, all my geraniums."

"Homer? He introduced himself? Well, his manners are certainly surpassing mine. I beg your pardon. I'm Joseph Bennett."

"Pleased to meet you," Kendra said dryly. "Your rabbit is a menace."

"There are two sides to every story, you know," Joseph said pleasantly. "In fairness we should make sure we have all the facts before we pass judgment on poor Homer, Miss...Mrs....?"

"Miss Kendra Smith," she said stiffly, "your neighbor. There are no facts to gather, Mr. Bennett. I saw Homer eat the geraniums. Well, one of them. The rest were already gobbled up."

"Call me Joseph, and I'll call you Kendra. That's the neighborly thing to do. Homer is guilty as sin, huh?"

"Definitely."

"Where were these geraniums?"

"In the greenhouse in my backyard."

A sudden wind whipped across the porch, and Kendra shivered.

"Why don't you step inside," Joseph said. "Coffee is hot. I have a few more questions regarding Homer's dastardly deed."

"Well, I..."

"You can bring your baseball bat," he said, grinning at her as he opened the screen door. "I wouldn't dream of attempting to ravish a woman as heavily armed as you are. Coffee?''

Kendra couldn't decide what to do. She was getting colder by the minute, and Joseph Bennett seemed nice enough. He was sexy beyond belief, but pleasant and neighborly. And she did want to make sure he'd replace the geraniums.

''Coming?'' Joseph asked.

''Yes, all right. One cup of coffee.'' Kendra stepped inside.

The cabin was a duplicate of Kendra's, right down to the same Early American furniture. The floors, however, were covered with a film of dust, and boxes and clothes were strewn everywhere.

''The kitchen is in better shape,'' Joseph said, leading the way. ''That's because I don't have much food yet. I arrived around midnight last night. I hope I didn't disturb your sleep.''

''I didn't hear a thing,'' Kendra said, sitting down at the kitchen table. Standing by the back door, Homer wiggled his nose at her. She glared at him. ''Aren't you cold?'' she asked Joseph. ''It's really nippy this morning.''

''Nope, I'm fine,'' he said, placing a mug in front of her, then sitting down opposite her. ''My mother is Italian. I'm very hot-blooded.''

I just *bet* he is, Kendra thought. Good grief, the man had sex appeal. She should rent him her baseball bat so he could fend off the women.

''Where's your bat?'' he asked.

''What? Oh, it's here, across my lap.''

Joseph chuckled and shook his head.

''About my geraniums,'' Kendra said, then took a sip of coffee.

"Ah, yes. Query: how did Homer get into your yard?"

"Through an opening in the fence."

"Which is the landlord's responsibility to maintain," Joseph said. "Therefore it is a hazardous nuisance when not in proper repair. I would say Homer is innocent of any wrongdoing with regard to passing through what he no doubt viewed as a legitimate passageway. Query: was the greenhouse door securely closed?"

"Well, no, it's warped, but—"

"Again, an invitation to enter. It would seem, Miss Kendra Smith, that you don't have much of a case against Homer."

"He ate my geraniums!"

"You saw him consuming only one. That he ate them all is conjecture on your part, and not admissible as evidence against the defendant."

"What are you, a lawyer?" Kendra was frowning.

"Yep," he said, lifting his mug. "A criminal trial lawyer. My client, Homer Bennett, is a victim of circumstances beyond his control. I move that this case be dismissed."

"I object!" Kendra exclaimed, smacking the table with her hand. "What about my flowers?"

"Can you supply sworn affidavits from reliable witnesses stating that you did indeed own six geraniums prior to this event?"

"No, but—"

"It's your word against Homer's." He smiled at her. "I'm prepared to produce character witnesses on Homer's behalf."

Kendra leaned forward and narrowed her eyes. "I don't know how to break this to you, Perry Mason, but you're a loony-tune."

Joseph put his head back and roared with laughter, great, booming laughter that seemed to bounce off the walls of the small room. It was an infectious sound, and Kendra found herself smiling. Homer hopped out of the kitchen and disappeared.

"Say now," Joseph said, "that is one lovely smile you have there, Kendra. You should smile every minute you're awake."

"That's not very realistic."

"No, I guess it isn't," he said, suddenly serious. "Not for anyone. Life doesn't work that way."

Their eyes met and held. The moment stretched on, and a strange tension began to curl through the air like smoke spiraling from a freshly lit fire. Kendra's heart began beating wildly. She felt pinned in place by Joseph's dark, dark eyes.

Then he shifted his gaze to her mouth. Kendra couldn't help but wonder what it would be like to have his lips pressed to hers, to have him draw her to his hard chest and . . . Saints above, what was she doing?

"Well—" she tore her gaze from his and stared into her mug "—you're obviously a very good lawyer, fast on your feet." Her voice was steady, wasn't it? It didn't sound very steady to her. "I assume you're on vacation."

"Sort of," he said gruffly, then took a big sip of coffee.

"It's rather late in the season for a lakeside vacation," she pointed out.

"*You're* here," he said.

"Oh, I live here. Well, at least I have since August. I teach school in Bay City."

"That's twenty miles away. Wouldn't it be simpler to live in Bay City? Besides, I'd think that a beautiful young woman like you would prefer the excitement of a bigger town. There can't be much to do here in Port Payne."

"It's extremely peaceful. So far, I like it very much."

"To each his own," Joseph said, shrugging.

"In all types of things," she said, "including one's choice of a pet."

"I take it you're referring to Homer." He was grinning. "My nephew won him at a carnival when Homer was no bigger than a mouse. My sister threw a conniption fit, and I said I'd find a pet shop or someplace to take him. Then I got involved in a long trial, and by the time it was over, Homer was my housekeeper's fair-haired boy—or rabbit, if you will. Homer thought he was the family cat. He's a year old now. He's a nifty little guy."

"He eats geraniums," Kendra said dryly.

"Don't you believe in leniency for first offenders?"

"No."

"Oh. Well, don't forget he was the victim of a hazardous nuisance. That is an innocent rabbit, madam." He put his hand up to demonstrate his sincerity.

"Hardly, counselor. Does he always go on vacation with you?"

"No, never, but my housekeeper is visiting her sister. Homer and I are lonely bachelors, winging it on our own."

Lonely? Kendra thought. Joseph Bennett wouldn't be lonely for long in Port Payne. Not once word spread that there was a handsome man on the loose. The lady bunnies would probably flock after Homer, too. The Bennett twosome would do all right for themselves, she thought.

"Have you been a teacher long?" Joseph asked pleasantly.

"This is my first year, which puts me rather behind schedule at twenty-six."

"You made a career change?"

"A lot of changes," Kendra told him, getting to her feet with her baseball bat in hand. "I must be going. Thank you for the coffee. I hope you enjoy your vacation. Will you be staying long?"

"It depends," he replied, walking beside her to the front door. "I'll see you soon, Kendra. After all, we *are* neighbors, with only a postage-stamp-size lawn separating us. I'm sure we'll bump into each other. Oh, I'll talk to the landlord about having the fence repaired."

"Good. I'd like to think that Homer's life of crime is at an end." She tried to keep a straight face.

"He's innocent, I tell you. Innocent."

They both laughed, and their eyes met. The smiles faded. Once again, Kendra lost track of time as she stared up into Joseph's dark eyes. The only sound she heard was the rapid thudding of her own heart.

"See you," he said finally.

"Yes." She hurried out the door.

Once she was within the safety of her own cabin, Kendra leaned back against the door. Her knees were trembling, and her heart was hammering. Joseph Bennett wasn't *that* overwhelming, she told herself. But oh, mercy, she'd been a goner as soon as she'd gazed into those inky eyes of his. And that smile. That body. Lord, he must be formidable in a courtroom. He was so big and powerful, and there was an unspoken authoritativeness about him. Once he got going in that rumbly voice of his, he'd have a jury under his spell. He'd have them eating out of the palm of his hand. She'd changed her mind. Joseph Bennett definitely was overwhelming and a man to be avoided.

Kendra pushed the image of Joseph firmly from her mind's eye and gathered her clothes for her Saturday trek to the laundromat in Port Payne. She'd shop for groceries, check her mail at the post office, then spend a quiet evening in front of the fire grading her students' papers. Her schedule had varied little since her arrival in Port Payne. It was a peaceful existence, just as she had said to Joseph.

Things were exactly the way she wanted them, and there was no room in her life for even lingering thoughts of Joseph Bennett and his off-the-wall rabbit. No room whatsoever.

"Hey," she said suddenly, "what about my geraniums? Homer is *not* innocent."

Port Payne was four blocks long and was comprised mostly of small craft shops offering unusual home-made items. At one end of the lakeside town were a grocery store, a gas station, a post office, a laundromat and other conventional establishments. But the remainder of the businesses relied on the summer tourist trade for their livelihood.

When Kendra had arrived in Port Payne, in August, it had been a beehive of activity. After Labor Day, there'd been an exodus back to larger towns and cities, and Port Payne had become quieter with each passing day. Many of the shops were now closed, the owners having returned to their city homes for the winter. Some of the local shopkeepers were year-round residents but counted on their summer income to see them through the lean months. They kept their shops open for business, but only in the hope that someone would drop by for coffee while the owner was busily at work replenishing the stock for the next summer.

Kendra changed from her baggy sweatshirt into a red sweater, pulled on her pea jacket and loaded her laundry into her car. When she arrived in town, she found the laundromat empty, and she spent the next two hours with her nose in a paperback novel while the machines hummed in the background. Once her basket of neatly folded wash was locked in the trunk of her compact car, she walked across the street to the post office.

"Hello, Kendra," an elderly woman said from behind the counter.

"Hello, Mrs. Howell." Kendra smiled. "Any mail for me?"

"Couple things." Mrs. Howell handed Kendra some envelopes. "You just missed seeing your new neighbor. Land's sake, he is a handsome boy. Polite, too. He said he'd be getting his mail here for a while and . . . mercy, he's a fine-looking young man."

Kendra laughed. "I've met Mr. Bennett. That *boy* must be thirty-five or -six years old."

"Perfect age for you, Kendra, and he's so handsome. You say you've already met him? That's marvelous, dear. Marvelous."

Kendra rolled her eyes heavenward, then glanced at her mail. A frown creased her brow when she saw a letter from her mother, and she put the envelopes in her purse.

"See you soon, Mrs. Howell," she said, heading for the door.

"You should bake a cake to welcome Joseph Bennett," Mrs. Howell told her. "It would be a neighborly thing to do. Do you hear me, Kendra?"

"I hear you. Bye," she called over her shoulder as she beat a hasty retreat.

Joseph Bennett had been to the grocery store, too, she learned.

"Nice young man," Mr. Frazier said as he rang up Kendra's groceries. "Said he'd already had the pleasure of meeting you."

"Yes, we've met," Kendra said.

Mr. Frazier was seventy if he was a day, and Kendra had yet to see him without his battered fishing hat firmly in place on his head. It was covered with hand-tied fishing flies, and Kendra spent her time in the checkout line peering at the brightly colored assortment.

"He's up from Detroit, you know," Mr. Frazier told her.

"What?" Kendra drew her gaze from his hat.

"That Joseph Bennett is up from Detroit. Said he didn't know how long he'd be staying. I told him at least he was used to the cold."

"He's very hot-blooded," Kendra said. Oh, no, why had she blurted *that* out?

"That a fact, now?" Mr. Frazier was squinting at her over the top of his glasses, a big grin on his wrinkled face.

"What I mean is—" Kendra felt a warm flush on her face "—he mentioned that he's half-Italian and he doesn't feel the cold, or some such thing." She threw her hands up in exasperation. "I don't know!"

"Well, that explains why he bought all the fixings for spaghetti. Suppose he'll invite you over for home-cooked spaghetti, Kendra?"

"I doubt that, Mr. Frazier. How much do I owe you?"

"I told Joseph Bennett that you were new here from California, and we were hoping you wouldn't hightail it home first time it snowed."

"I won't do that," she said, smiling. "My contract is for the entire school year in Bay City."

"Well, it'll be fine having you here for the winter, Kendra. Don't get young people in Port Payne past Labor Day. Now, if that Joseph would stay on—"

"Mr. Frazier," Kendra interrupted him, "my bill?"

Joseph Bennett had been to every store in town, she discovered. Kendra heard a glowing report from the McCauley twins, spinster ladies in their sixties who ran the drugstore. Bubbling with excitement, they told Kendra that Joseph Bennett was just "the cutest thing" they'd ever seen, and didn't Kendra think it would be friendly of her to give him a personal tour of Port Payne? Kendra mumbled something she hoped was semiintelligent and hurried away.

"Good grief," she muttered when she was safely outside. Joseph Bennett certainly had created a stir. But there'd been a flurry of excitement when the locals learned that Kendra was staying on through the winter, she reminded herself. Apparently any change in routine in Port Payne past Labor Day was a newsworthy event. However, the dear old souls of that sleepy little town had better forget their matchmaking hopes for her and Joseph. Kendra was not interested.

"Kendra! Hello, Kendra!"

Kendra glanced up to see a woman waving at her from across the street.

"Hi, Libby," Kendra called, smiling.

"Come have a cup of tea."

"Wonderful." Kendra's smile widened. "I'm on my way."

Libby St. Simon, an attractive redhead in her late thirties, owned an exquisite shop that specialized in stained-glass creations. She did all her own work and made small sun catchers and wind chimes for the tourist trade. Widowed for five years, she owned a home in Midland as well as one in Port Payne and divided her time between the two. While in Midland she contracted for larger projects, such as stained-glass windows and door panels. She was friendly and outgoing, and Kendra enjoyed her company.

"It's getting nippy," Libby said, waving Kendra into the shop. "I have some tea made. Come in back. *And* tell me all about Joseph Bennett."

"Not you, too," Kendra moaned, following Libby to the cozy back room. Kendra slipped off her jacket and sat in a rocker by the Ben Franklin stove.

"Well, of course me, too," Libby said, laughing. "I saw him out the window, then called Mrs. Howell to find out who he was. I'm practicing to be old and nosy. Port Payne is all in a dither. Joseph Bennett is known officially as Kendra's neighbor."

"I don't suppose anyone stopped to consider that Mr. Anderson's cabins are the only ones around the lake that have been winterized. Where else would Joseph stay?"

Libby handed her a mug of tea. "But do note that there are eight of those cabins. Mr. Anderson put Joseph right next to you. Bless their hearts," she said, sitting in another rocker, "these folks do love a romance."

"There's not going to be a romance between Joseph Bennett and me," Kendra said crossly. "Don't people around here have anything better to do than play cupid?"

"Nope," Libby said, laughing. "Not in the winter. I swear, Kendra, that Joseph is gorgeous."

"Help yourself. He's all yours."

"I might be tempted, but I'm still seeing my doctor friend in Midland. Listen, it would do you good to flirt a little, get Joseph to ask you out to dinner, have a night on the town in Bay City."

"No, Libby, I'm perfectly content with the way I have things arranged in my life."

"Yes, yes, it's peaceful. But you've been peaceful for nearly two months now. What harm would a dinner date do?"

"You and I went to dinner in Bay City," Kendra pointed out.

"We are discussing a very sexy man here. Pay attention."

"No."

"Lordy, you're stubborn. I'm not asking you to marry the guy. Just go out with him."

"That's what my mother said, and look how that turned out."

"Well, from what you've told me, you were a different person then. You didn't know how to do anything but try to please your parents, even to the point of marrying Jack the Jerk. But that's all behind you now. You're an independent woman with your own life and career. There's no reason in the world why you shouldn't date, starting with someone like Joseph Bennett.''

"No," she said firmly.

"Well, damn." Libby was frowning now. "You're no fun. I'm not giving up on you, though."

"Let's change the subject. Are you staying for the weekend?"

"No, I'm driving back to Midland. I have a date with my doc. Date, Kendra—as in with a handsome man, dinner out, dancing. Fabulous. You really should consider working it into your peaceful routine. Now, Joseph looks like he'd be some kind of date. Whew! What a body. Build a cozy fire, then—"

"I've got to go." Kendra jumped to her feet. "I have groceries in the car. I'll see you next time you come to Port Payne."

Libby got up to see Kendra out. "At least think about going out with Joseph."

"Libby, what makes you so sure he'd even ask me?"

"Are you crazy? You're a beautiful woman, Kendra. Why should he go to Bay City to case the singles bars when he's next door to a lovely lady?"

"Oh, good grief," Kendra said, shrugging into her jacket.

"I still say he'd be a helluva date," Libby muttered, staring off into space. "If it weren't for my darling doc... Nope, Joseph is yours. I'll expect a full report when I come back."

"There will be nothing to report beyond the fact that I might have murdered his rabbit."

"What?" Libby looked utterly confused.

"It's a long, ridiculous story. See you, Libby. Bye."

"Shape up your act!" Libby hollered after her. "Peacefulness is boring!"

"Brother," Kendra groaned, then marched to her car.

Kendra was frowning as she drove toward the cabin. Peacefulness was not boring, she told herself. It was peaceful. She'd had enough of frantic living, of parties, of social events that had to be attended because it was the proper thing to do. She'd lived in an affluent, privileged world and followed its rules to the letter. And she'd nearly lost herself in the process. She wanted to be by herself, answering her own needs, doing as she pleased. She just wanted to be left alone.

Joseph's car was parked next to his cabin, and Kendra gave it and the cabin a glare before turning into her own driveway. Her Saturday jaunt into Port Payne had been jarring because of Joseph, and she was in no mood to have her life disrupted.

A rumble of thunder greeted her as she stepped out of the car, and she glanced up at the sky to see storm clouds gathering rapidly. She reached back across the seat, grabbed a bag of groceries and hurried toward the cabin, hoping to have her car unloaded before the heavens opened up. She had one foot on the first step leading to the porch when she saw them.

Six pots. Six pots, containing six red geraniums in full bloom were lined up across her porch.

"Oh, my," Kendra gasped. She pulled a note from one of the pots. "I'm sorry. Homer," she read aloud, then burst into laughter.

Kendra stared at the cabin next door for several seconds before a clap of thunder snapped her out of her trance. She stepped over the row of flowers and went inside. A few minutes later the geraniums were lined up in the living room beneath the window. Kendra was still smiling. She unloaded the car, put away the perishable groceries, then glanced up at the sky before running to Joseph's cabin.

"Hi," he said when he opened the door in answer to her knock.

"Hello." Kendra smiled up at him. "May I speak to Homer, please?"

"Certainly," he told her solemnly, though his eyes sparkled with amusement. "Do come in."

"Thank you." She stepped inside.

"I'll get Homer. However, if he's meditating, I won't be able to disturb him."

"I understand perfectly."

Kendra watched as Joseph disappeared in the direction of the bedroom. How could a man look sexier fully dressed, she wondered, than he had half-naked? It was amazing, but Joseph Bennett in faded jeans and a black crew-neck sweater was something to behold. His tan appeared darker now, as did his thick black hair and his eyes. There was an aura of sensuality surrounding Joseph like nothing she had ever encountered before. He was disconcerting, to say the least, and a tad frightening. She would speak with Homer, then get the heck out of there.

"Here he is," Joseph announced, coming back into the room with Homer tucked under his arm. "Shedding all over my sweater."

"Hello, Homer," Kendra greeted the rabbit, trying to restrain a smile. "I wanted to thank you for the beautiful geraniums and the nice note."

Homer wiggled his nose.

"He's terribly sorry, you know," Joseph said. "Oh, I fixed the fence myself, so that problem is solved."

"I really do thank you for the flowers, Joseph," she told him, smiling up at him.

"I was surprised I could find them in Port Payne."
He set Homer on the floor and looked down at himself. "Now I own a furry sweater. Anyway, I took a little tour of the town. Nice people, friendly. They certainly speak highly of you, Kendra. Your name was mentioned everywhere I went."

"Well, you have to understand that there's not much to do here after Labor Day. Everyone was talking about you, too. You caused a lot of excitement in Port Payne. Just don't pay any attention if they... Well, they're very dear people, but..." She sputtered to a stop.

"Are you saying they might attempt a bit of matchmaking between us?" He grinned at her.

"It's a distinct possibility. Hopefully they'll give up once they realize it isn't going to work."

"It isn't?" he inquired, raising his dark eyebrows.

"Of course not."

"Oh. Well, we are going to be friendly neighbors, aren't we? Is there a jealous man in your life who wouldn't want you borrowing a cup of sugar from me?"

"No, there's no one, but—"

"Good. That solves another problem."

"Problem?"

"The spaghetti. I'm making the sauce, or gravy as my Italian mama calls it. I'm using her special recipe. Thing is, it makes a big batch, and there's no room in my freezer to store it."

"Cut the recipe in half," she suggested.

"No can do. I've already chopped up most of the stuff. So the solution is for you to come over for dinner tonight. Seven o'clock?"

"Oh, well, I don't think—"

"Do you already have a date?"

"No, I was going to grade papers, but—"

"Great. I really appreciate this, Kendra. If you eat a hefty serving, it will mean Homer and I won't have spaghetti for three meals a day all next week."

"Homer eats spaghetti?"

"Well, sure. I told him he was half-Italian, like me, and he believed me. Dumb rabbit."

Kendra laughed.

"Seven o'clock?" Joseph asked.

"Yes. Yes, all right," she finally said, smiling and shaking her head. "You win."

Suddenly Joseph became very serious. "Usually I do, if I put my mind to it. I can be very tenacious. It's a matter of deciding how badly I want something."

Or someone? Kendra thought as she gazed into Joseph's eyes. What defense would a woman have against Joseph Bennett if he were set on a course of seduction? Oh, for heaven's sake, she admonished herself, there was nothing seductive about spaghetti.

"What can I bring to dinner?" she asked.

"Just you," Joseph said, his voice low as he trailed his thumb lightly over her cheek. "Just bring yourself, Kendra Smith."

Two

___

Kendra managed to escape with the explanation that she didn't want to be caught in a downpour. Safely inside her own cabin, she lit a fire, then relaxed on the sofa. As if moving of their own volition, her fingertips drifted to her cheek, where Joseph's callused thumb had seemed to blaze a heated path across her skin.

She was acting ridiculous, Kendra fumed. She was a twenty-six-year-old divorcée, for Pete's sake, not some dewy-eyed teenager. She'd been married for two years, then spent the past two years since her divorce buried in textbooks as she completed her college education. Now, for the first time in her life, she was functioning on her own, making her own decisions, determining her own destiny, a destiny that did not include coming unglued because a virile man had touched her cheek.

"Ludicrous," she told herself, staring into the fire. Her reactions to Joseph were absurd, to say the least.

Well, now she was back in control. Sharing pasta with a man who used a rabbit as a chaperon did not a romantic interlude make. Fine, she thought, getting to her feet.

Kendra finished putting away the groceries, placed the clean clothes in her closet and drawers, then washed the kitchen floor as rain beat on the roof. The only heat in the cabin in addition to the fireplace was a panel ray unit in the larger bedroom, which had one temperature: hot. The night she had used it, she had felt as though she were smothering and had developed a roaring headache. Her plan was to stay in front of the fire through the winter evenings, then dive beneath a tower of blankets on the bed when it was time to go to sleep.

Kendra checked the soil for moisture in the geranium pots, then stood staring down at the bright red blossoms. Joseph's image flitted in front of her eyes, and her fingers once again crept to her cheek. She looked out the window, hardly able to see more than a few feet beyond the cabin as the rain continued to fall in a heavy torrent. She felt a sudden chill, and hugged herself tightly.

It was as though the rain had cut her off from the world, she mused. She was totally alone, and for the first time since she'd come to Port Payne, she had a niggling sense of loneliness. No, she wasn't lonely, Kendra told herself firmly. It was understandable that she'd have to adjust to her new life-style. All she had to do was remember the plastic world she'd lived in for so long to reaffirm that this was where she wanted to be. No, she wasn't lonely, only alone. And that was how she wanted it.

Despite what Joseph had said, Kendra decided she really should take something to add to the meal that night. Even if he had the menu planned, Joseph could save her offering for another time. Everyone liked chocolate-chip cookies. Did rabbits like chocolate-chip cookies? she wondered. Rabbits who ate spaghetti probably did.

Kendra went into the kitchen, her momentary gloom forgotten until she saw her purse sitting on the table. With a sigh she sank onto a chair and pulled out the two letters she'd been given by Mrs. Howell. One was a notice of a private fashion show to be held at an exclusive boutique in Beverly Hills. Kendra barely glanced at it before she threw it away. Then she slowly opened the other letter, which was from her mother.

The weekly sermon, she thought ruefully, scanning the scented paper. In it her mother told Kendra she should come to her senses and return to California, where she belonged. Her show of independence was nothing more than a childish tantrum, and no one was impressed. She went on to tell Kendra that she was a Beverly Hills Smith and should be taking her place in the social climate her parents had worked so hard for. She was somebody of affluence and importance.

"A Smith," Kendra murmured, shaking her head. Only her mother could act as if the name Smith were as recognizable as Kennedy or Rockefeller. Well, too bad. She wasn't going back. She'd found the place she wanted to be, and she was staying. And she had chocolate-chip cookies to make!

Why she suddenly felt lighthearted, Kendra didn't know. She was actually humming. It was understandable that Joseph's image floated constantly through her mind, she decided. After all, she was making the cookies for him, for a criminal trial lawyer with a pet rabbit that thought it was a cat. What an unusual, intriguing man Joseph Bennett was. How long was he going to stay in Port Payne? Not that it mattered, of course, but it would be pleasant to have a neighbor for a while.

A friendly neighbor, Kendra told herself as she broke eggs into a bowl. That's all she wanted a man like Joseph to be, a friend. She had no intention of being a handsome man's vacation fling. She'd been knocked off kilter by his virile good looks and raw sensuality, but that was over. She'd regained her equilibrium. Goodness, it felt terrific to be in charge of one's own life, she marveled.

The cabin was soon filled with the aroma of freshly baked cookies, and Kendra ate a handful with a glass of milk. She arranged a stack of the treats on a plate, covered it with foil, then cleaned the kitchen. She curled up on the sofa in front of the fire with a book, having decided that she'd grade her students' papers tomorrow. The rain slackened, then finally stopped, leaving the sky overcast and the air chilly.

Just before seven, Kendra stood on tiptoe to glimpse as much of herself as possible in the mirror over the bathroom sink. Her tan suede slacks were expensive and fit her well. The rich silk of her dark brown blouse hugged her full breasts, and her hair was a cascade of blond waves falling to her shoulders. Her makeup was sparely and expertly applied, and her blue eyes were sparkling as she slipped on the suede jacket that matched her slacks. She felt alive, bursting with energy, and knew she looked attractive. She was about to spend the evening in the company of a handsome man, her friendly neighbor, and the hours ahead held great appeal.

Kendra double-checked the ashes in the fireplace to be sure they were cool, picked up the plate of cookies and went out the door.

"Oh, ugh," she said a few moments later. The heels of her brown pumps sank into the wet grass, and irrationally she wondered if she was stuck there for life. She wiggled free, then tiptoed across the lawn, feeling like a thief in the night. "I should have taken a taxi," she muttered.

Joseph opened the door almost as soon as she knocked, and Kendra felt her heart begin to pound as she looked up at him. There were no lamps on in the living room; the only light came from a roaring fire. Joseph stood in the shadows of the almost eerie light that outlined his massive frame. He appeared taller, broader than he had before, and strangely threatening. Kendra knew she couldn't have spoken at that moment if her life had depended on it.

"Hello, Kendra," Joseph said, his voice low. "Come in where it's warm."

Said the spider to the fly, Kendra thought, swallowing a nearly hysterical giggle. Darn it, she was flustered again. What was it about this man?

She smiled weakly and stepped into the living room. "I brought you some chocolate-chip cookies," she said. "You have to share them with Homer, though."

Joseph chuckled, and Kendra silently moaned as she felt a funny flutter in the pit of her stomach.

"Thank you," he said, taking the plate from her. "I can't speak for Homer, but I'm crazy about chocolate-chip cookies. Kendra, you look beautiful. Absolutely beautiful."

"Why, thank you, Joseph." Good. She'd sounded slightly bored and ultrasophisticated. "So do you." What? Darn. So much for sophistication.

Joseph chuckled again. Kendra decided she wanted to go home.

"Would you like a glass of wine?" Joseph asked.

"Yes, thank you."

"Have a seat in front of the fire. I'll be right back," he said, smiling at her.

Kendra nodded and watched as Joseph went into the kitchen. He was dressed in black slacks and a black V-neck sweater over an open-necked pale blue shirt. Kendra stared at the entire gorgeous length of his retreating form, then sank onto the sofa.

So far, not so good, she thought ruefully. Well, what did she expect? All her life she'd been sheltered, pampered, watched over and cared for. Oh, she'd traveled extensively in Europe, hobnobbed with the rich and famous, jet-setted from here to there. But never alone. At her wedding she'd felt like a cocker spaniel being handed over to its new owner.

"Here you are," Joseph said, coming back into the room. He handed her a juice glass filled with dark red wine. "Not fancy, but it's a decent wine." He sat down next to her. "A toast," he went on, lifting his glass. "To my lovely neighbor. To you, Kendra Smith."

Kendra touched her glass to Joseph's and took a sip, but didn't look at him. He had shifted to face her, his thigh brushing hers. She was acutely aware of the heat, the muscled strength of Joseph's leg, and stared into her glass as though it were the most fascinating thing she had ever seen.

"Kendra," Joseph said quietly, "I get the distinct impression that I'm making you nervous."

"No. No, I . . ."

"Would you like to go home and get your baseball bat?"

Kendra abruptly looked up at Joseph, fully expecting him to be laughing at her. But he wasn't. He was gazing at her with a warmth, a tenderness, she would not have thought him capable of.

She couldn't help but smile.

"No," Kendra said, then laughed softly, "I don't think I'll need my baseball bat tonight."

"Good." He nodded. "You're a scary lady when you're toting that thing. I was shaking in my shoes."

"I can't picture you being afraid of anything," Kendra said, still smiling.

"Why? Because I'm a man and I'm big? I doubt I'd be afraid going up against another man, but there are many kinds of fear."

"Yes, that's true, but—"

"Sit tight," he said, getting to his feet. "I've got to check my sauce."

"It smells delicious."

"Just remember you promised to eat a ton. You're saving Homer and me from spaghetti for breakfast."

"Where is Homer?"

"He's all worn out," Joseph said as he headed for the kitchen. "We had to whip this place into shape today for our special dinner guest. He's dead to the world. I'll be right back."

There are many kinds of fear, Kendra said to herself, repeating Joseph's words. What could a man like him possibly be afraid of? She had to admit she'd been guilty of assuming that a man of his size and apparent strength was in complete control of his life. She had so much to learn about so many things.

"Kendra," Joseph called from the kitchen. "We're ready to dig in."

Kendra smiled as she got to her feet and went inside. "What can I do to help?"

"Would you get the salad out of the refrigerator while I get the French bread out of the oven?"

A few minutes later they were seated at the small table. The salad was crisp, and the spaghetti delicious. Kendra complimented the chef.

"Thank you, ma'am," he said, smiling. "My mother insisted we all know how to make sauce from scratch using her own special recipe. One by one, she'd stand us on a chair and give instructions."

"One by one? How many of you are there?"

"Eight. Four girls, four boys. I'm the third child, first boy," he said matter-of-factly.

"What a marvelous family."

"Noisy family. What a zoo. But it was great. We lived in a big old weather-beaten house near Detroit with tall trees and a huge yard. We fought, squabbled like hell, but we loved one another. No one messed with the Bennett sisters, or they'd end up dealing with the Bennett brothers. Oh, we were tough." He chuckled softly. "We'd wear those sunglasses with the mirror lenses, roll up the sleeves of our T-shirts, then go stalking the poor joker who had dared insult one of our sisters."

"Did your mother know what you were doing?"

"Sure. She's the one who bought us the sunglasses. She said Italian men were honor-bound to protect their women."

"And your father?" Kendra asked, smiling warmly.

"He'd just shake his head and laugh. He said not to call him if we landed in jail. Nothing fazed my father. Someone had to stay calm, since my mother is very volatile. As the first son, I was named after my father. He's always been good ole Joe Bennett, so I was always called Joseph to cut down on the confusion.''

"It sounds as though you had a wonderful childhood." There was a wistful note in her voice.

"First-rate."

"Then why... Well, it's none of my business, but I'd think you'd want a family like that of your own someday."

"I do. I honestly do. But I guess time just got away from me while I was establishing my career. A lot of things got away from me." He was frowning.

"What do you mean?"

"Enough about me," Joseph said abruptly. "Say, did you see the reviews on that new movie starring..."

The remainder of the meal passed in comfortable conversation about movies, books and other innocuous topics. Kendra relaxed more and more. She was happy to find that Joseph was prepared to listen to her ideas, consider her opinions, then launch into a vigorous and enjoyable debate if he didn't agree.

During a rare silence, Kendra glanced up to see Joseph looking at her intently.

"Is something wrong?" she asked.

"Not at all. I was just realizing that we've discussed everything but you. Tell me all about Miss Kendra Smith. I swear, they didn't have beautiful teachers like you when I was in school. I hear you're from California. How did you end up in Port Payne?"

"The teaching position in Bay City was advertised nationwide, and I flew out to interview for it. I got the job, took a few extra days to explore the area and discovered Port Payne. I rented the cottage, flew home, loaded up my car, and here I am."

"Why?"

"Pardon me?" His question had caught her off guard.

"Why are you in a place like this? Why is this your first year of teaching at age twenty-six? Who are you, Kendra?" he demanded, looking directly into her eyes.

"I'm me, pure and simple. Nothing fancy."

"Oh?" He cocked an eyebrow. "There's nothing fancy about a five-hundred-dollar suede suit and a hundred-dollar silk blouse? There's an elegance about you, too, a certain gracefulness that says social status, old money. You seem to forget that I'm a trial lawyer. I have an eye for detail, and I've got to be able to make sound judgments regarding what I see and hear. I repeat my question: Who are you, Kendra?"

"Did it ever occur to you," Kendra asked, her voice tight, "that it's none of your business?"

"Well, sure," he said, grinning at her, "but how am I going to find out all about you if I don't ask?"

"I'm not in the habit of telling my life history to someone I hardly know."

"Hey, you know me. I'm your neighbor; my rabbit ate your geraniums; you're sampling the secret spaghetti sauce of the Bennett clan," he said, listing each accomplishment by counting it on his fingers. "Where in California did you live?"

"Beverly Hills."

"That fits. Go on."

"Darn it, Joseph, I feel as though I'm on the witness stand."

"You do? I'm sorry. Habit, I guess. I didn't mean to pin you to the wall. I'm sincerely interested in finding out about you, who you are, why you're here. You're a fascinating woman, as well as a beautiful one."

"Fascinating?" she repeated, laughing suddenly. "That is the last word I would've chosen to describe myself."

"But it's true. At first glance you give the impression of being poised, sophisticated, in charge. But then... I don't know exactly. There's a vulnerability about you, a sense of fragility, wariness... an underlying fear of some sort. How can I say this?" He looked off to the side, thinking. "You remind me of a skittish fawn who isn't sure where danger might lie."

Emotions seemed to tumble through Kendra, like streams rushing forward to spill together in a churning swirl in the pit of her stomach. She was angry that Joseph would be so bold, so presumptuous. She felt frightened, stripped bare, as though he had delved deep inside her to view her very soul. And she was filled with joy to think that at last—*at last*—someone had looked beneath the surface to find the flesh-and-blood human being she was.

She stared at Joseph, not knowing what might be evident from her expression, not knowing what he might see.

"Your eyes." He covered her hand with his, and his voice was low as he spoke. "Your eyes mirror your feelings. I see so much there, Kendra—anger, fear and a flicker of something warm and gentle. You can turn a man inside out with those blue eyes. Talk to me. Tell me who you are."

"I was lost," she said, her voice hushed, "and now I've found myself. I come from a very wealthy socially prominent family, and I lived a very glamorous life. I was, as my mother likes to say, one of the Beverly Hills Smiths. Then I was Mrs. Jack Florence, playing the role of the executive's wife to the hilt. Now I'm Miss Kendra Smith, schoolteacher, person, woman. I'm nothing more or less than you see before you, Joseph."

"What I see—" he was smiling gently "—is a lovely young woman."

"Who's taking her first steps alone," she said, her voice stronger as she lifted her chin. "I didn't run away. I turned my back, squared my shoulders and walked out the door, shutting it on a world that was empty and cold, plastic and phony."

"And I bet your family is mad as hell."

"Furious." She managed a smile. "I'm in a phase, you see, throwing a tantrum," she said wryly. "They're clicking their tongues, shaking their heads and waiting impatiently for me to come to my senses."

"Including your ex-husband?"

"Oh, no, not Jack," she said, slowly pulling her hand free. "He remarried a few months after I divorced him two years ago. He needed a wife to run his home and attend all the right social functions while he climbed the corporate ladder."

"Did you love him?"

"Jack? No," she admitted, a trace of sadness in her voice. "I didn't particularly enjoy the endless parties, gala balls, the shopping jaunts to Paris and London, either. I realize I'm sitting here in a very expensive suit, but I didn't think about the cost of it when I put it on. It's attractive and comfortable, so I wore it. I wasn't trying to impress you with the quality of it. I don't know how to explain all this to you so that it makes sense. I was a dutiful daughter who did all that was expected of her. And then I stopped."

"That was an incredibly brave thing to do."

"No, I'm not brave," she said, shaking her head. "I'm scared to death that someone will find out I have no idea what I'm doing. I had a flat tire one day, and I just stood there like an idiot waiting for someone to show up and fix it. It finally dawned on me that it was up to me to handle the situation. I balanced my checkbook myself for the first time last week. Well, it didn't balance, but it was close."

"Good for you," he said. "Miss Lost and Found Smith, I'd say you're doing fine. First steps are always shaky, Kendra. You may stumble a bit, but you've got to hang in there. I admire and respect you for what you're doing."

"Oh, well, thank you," she stammered, blushing slightly.

"Now! Take that last bite of spaghetti, before it gets cold. Rule one of the Bennett house: you always clean your plate."

"Yes, sir," she said and laughed.

Kendra insisted on helping with the dishes. When the kitchen was set to order, Joseph turned off the kitchen light and suggested they have a glass of wine in front of the fire.

"I won't eat for a week," Kendra groaned, collapsing on the sofa.

Joseph chuckled, then placed another log on the flames. The fire sent an orange glow over the darkened living room. Homer, who had finally reappeared, plopped down on the braided rug in front of the hearth and went to sleep.

Joseph finished his wine, set the glass on the mantel, then sat next to Kendra, spreading his arms out along the back of the sofa. She glanced at him and saw the faraway look on his face as he stared into the flames. She placed her glass on the end table and gazed into the fire. The minutes passed.

"Lost and found," Joseph finally said quietly. Kendra jumped at the sound of his deep voice. "I keep thinking about the way you phrased that," he said, turning to look at her. "It says it all, doesn't it? How many people get lost but never find themselves? Some play games and pretend everything is fine."

"It's easier that way at times," Kendra told him. "Lord knows I did that for years. I just couldn't take it anymore. So, here I am."

"And I'm glad." His voice was even lower. He lifted one hand to touch the silken strands of her hair. "Your hair looks like spun gold in the firelight."

Kendra looked at him, and their eyes met. It was a moment not measured in time. The sound of Kendra's heartbeat echoed in her ears. As the pressure of Joseph's hand on the back of her head increased, she knew he was going to kiss her. A tingle of excitement swept through her, nudging aside any fear.

Slowly, slowly, Joseph lowered his head to brush his lips over Kendra's in a soft, fleeting motion. Then he brought his other hand to the back of her neck and took full possession of her mouth. His tongue trailed along her bottom lip, seeking and then gaining entry to the sweet darkness within her mouth. She slid her hands up his chest and felt the rich material of his sweater and the steely muscles beneath. Her eyes drifted closed as she savored the sensation of Joseph's lips on hers, his tongue dueling seductively with hers. She tasted him, inhaled his aroma, took his heat into herself.

Joseph raised his head a fraction of an inch, then claimed Kendra's mouth again. As she lifted her arms to encircle his neck, his arms dropped to her waist and his hands moved inside her jacket, then upward to her silk-covered back. He shifted his weight slightly to bring her to him.

Sensations rocketed through Kendra: the sweet pain of her breasts pressed to the unyielding wall of Joseph's chest; a coiling, pulsing heat deep within her; the tingling awareness of her entire body. She felt gloriously alive and free. Desire blossomed within her, and a soft moan rose in her throat.

"Ah, Kendra," Joseph said, his voice raspy. He slid his hands slowly from her back, then gripped her shoulders, moving her gently away from him. He looked into her eyes, then drew a steadying breath. "Your eyes are nearly gray," he said, trailing his thumb over her cheek. "Damn, I want to go on kissing you. You taste so good, feel so good in my arms."

"Yes," she murmured, her own voice unsteady, "so do you." She continued to gaze up at him, then ran her tongue over her kiss-swollen bottom lip.

"Damn," Joseph groaned. Then his mouth came down hard on hers.

As Joseph's tongue plunged deep into Kendra's mouth, he pushed her jacket from her shoulders and down her arms. The rush of cool air felt heavenly against her heated skin, as did Joseph's hands roaming over the silken material of her blouse. She sank her fingers into his thick hair to pull his mouth down harder on hers.

Warnings of danger screamed in Kendra's mind, but she ignored them. She wanted, needed, this moment. The feel of Joseph's mouth on hers and the tempestuous sensations it created within her body were like nothing she'd ever experienced. A wondrous trembling rippled through her as she drank of his heady taste and surrounded herself with his strength. He cupped her breasts, then trailed his thumbs over the tautening buds beneath her blouse.

It was all so wrong, but Kendra didn't care. She gloried in her own femininity and relished the power of Joseph's masculinity. It was ecstasy, and she didn't want it to end.

Joseph managed to drag his lips from hers. "Kendra," he murmured, "I've got to stop."

"What?" she said, blinking once.

"Lord, those eyes of yours are telling me so much." His voice was harsh with passion. "You want me as much as I want you."

"Oh, I . . . Well . . ."

"I know," he said. "Too much, too fast." He moved a few inches away from her on the couch, and, drawing a deep, shuddering breath as she stared into the fire, he whispered, "I know."

Dear heaven, what had she done? Kendra thought. She'd kissed Joseph Bennett like . . . darn it, like a woman. She'd kissed him because she'd wanted to, because it felt right and good and had made her feel alive and special. She refused, absolutely refused, to feel guilty for the pleasure she'd experienced in his arms.

"I bet you wish you'd brought your baseball bat," Joseph said, still staring into the flames.

"No," she answered. And then she laughed softly.

Joseph turned his head to look at her and frowned.

"Do you think I'm angry or upset?" she asked. "I was a willing participant in those kisses. I'm not a child, you know. I make my own decisions."

"No, you're not a child," he said, sighing. He leaned back and stretched his arms along the top of the sofa again. "Not exactly."

"What do you mean?" She was frowning slightly.

"Have you been with a man other than your husband?" he demanded, turning to look at her.

"Well, for heaven's sake, what a rude question! And none of your business, I might add."

"I think you haven't. I think you shared a marriage bed with a man you didn't love, and I'd bet twenty bucks that the sex was lousy."

"You have a lot of nerve." Kendra jumped to her feet.

"Hold it," he ordered, his hand shooting out to grab her wrist. "This is important."

Kendra settled back stiffly on the cushion, then looked pointedly at Joseph's large hand holding her wrist. He released her, and she glared at him.

"Displays of machismo don't impress me, Mr. Bennett," she said coolly.

"Kendra, I'm trying to do the decent thing here, and you're really pushing me."

"Well, excuse me!" She crossed her arms over her breasts. "Since when is discussing my sex life, my experience or lack of same, the decent thing to do? What it is, is nosy. You'll fit into the Port Payne populace fine. You have just the right personality for it."

"Oh, you're asking for it," he said, narrowing his eyes.

"What's next? You put on your sunglasses and do your Italian hit-man routine?"

"Damn it, shut up and listen to me! Believe me, Kendra Smith, I'm very aware that you are a woman. But might I point out that I am a man? Not a monk—a man."

"So?"

"So I've been around the block a few times. You, Kendra, are seducible. We could have been in my bed right now if I hadn't called a halt."

"Don't be ridiculous," she said, then sniffed indignantly.

"Were you aware that I took off your jacket?"

"Of course. It was too warm to wear in front of the fire anyway."

"I see. And is that why you've failed to close the two buttons I undid on your blouse?"

Kendra's hand flew to her blouse, and she looked down in wide-eyed horror.

"Oh . . ." she said, redoing the buttons with shaking hands. "I didn't realize that you'd... What I mean is... Oh."

"I rest my case," he said, his voice gentling. "Yes, you're a woman. A very beautiful, desirable one. I want you. I want to make love to you, and with you. But when that happens, I don't want you to be sorry. You're emerging from a sheltered cocoon to take those first steps we talked about. I sure as hell don't know where all this grand nobility of mine is coming from, but it's there. I can't have you. Not yet."

"Not yet?" she said, jumping to her feet. "What are you going to do, pencil it in on your calendar? You're arrogant. Do you know that? I have no intention of going to bed with you. Ever."

In one smooth, powerful motion Joseph was on his feet, gripping her shoulders and claiming her mouth. Her eyes widened in shock, then drifted closed in the next instant as the ember of desire within her instantly burst into flame. She leaned into him wanting, seeking more.

"Not yet," Joseph said, his voice rough as he lifted his head. "Damn, you're enough to drive a man straight out of his mind. I've never met anyone like you. You're woman and child mixed up together. What am I going to do with you?"

"Nothing." She snatched up her jacket. "Pretend I don't exist. Feed your spaghetti to your rabbit."

"Just ignore the fact that you live next door—right," he said sarcastically.

"Precisely." She threw her jacket over her shoulders.

"And you, Kendra?" His voice was low. "Can you ignore me? Can you ignore what you were feeling when I kissed you? You wanted me; I wanted you. This isn't going to end here, and you know it."

"It most certainly is," she stated, and walked toward the door.

Joseph crossed the room quickly and blocked her exit.

Kendra glared at him. "Move your big carcass."

"No. I want to ask you—"

"All right, all right." Kendra finally gave up. "No, I have not been with a man other than my husband. As to whether or not the sex was lousy, as you coarsely put it, I wouldn't know, because I have nothing to compare it to. Satisfied?"

"Well, I appreciate the information," he said, grinning at her. "However, that wasn't the question I was asking. I had decided you were right and it was none of my business."

"What!"

"I wanted to ask if you'd like to row out on the lake with me tomorrow. It shouldn't be too cold. What do you say?"

"We're not talking about sex," Kendra said, shaking her head slightly. "We're discussing boats?"

"Sure. It'll be fun. Well, you think about it, and I'll check with you tomorrow. Come on, I'll walk you home."

"I'm perfectly capable of—"

"Don't argue with a sexually frustrated Italian," Joseph said, opening the door to let her precede him out.

"I knew we were talking about sex," Kendra muttered.

Joseph chuckled and fell in step beside her. On the front porch, he shoved his hands into his pockets.

"Good night," he said pleasantly, rocking back and forth on the balls of his feet. "Front porches intimidate me. They remind me of my first dates, when I never knew if I should kiss her or not. To this day, I can't pucker up on a front porch."

Despite herself, Kendra laughed, though she wasn't sure why she was laughing.

"Thank you for the delicious dinner, Joseph."

"Thank you for...everything," he answered quietly. "I'll see you tomorrow."

"Good night," Kendra said, then went inside and closed the door behind her.

Three

The next morning, as Kendra ate breakfast, she decided that Joseph Bennett was most definitely a rude man. He was outspoken, nosy and brash. He'd quizzed her about her sexual experience as casually as if he were talking about the weather.

But, she told herself, Joseph was warm and fun, and he really listened to her when she spoke. He seemed genuinely interested in who she was as a person.

Later, while in the shower, Kendra admitted to herself that she had more than responded to Joseph's kiss and touch; she'd felt a flash of desire like none before. He was without a doubt the most masculine, most alluring man she had ever met. Being held in his arms had been wonderful; his kiss was beyond description. She'd savored each sensation that had rocketed through her when he'd kissed her. Joseph had made her feel alive and incredibly glad to be a woman.

As Kendra dressed in jeans and a pink sweater, she kept asking herself one question: Now what?

She'd better think this through a bit, she decided. Joseph was obviously very experienced in dealing with women. He'd informed Kendra that she was seducible and that she wanted him as much as he did her. He'd even assured her that it was guaranteed that they'd make love.

"Rude, very rude man," Kendra muttered. But she knew he was probably right. Jack had been a perfect gentleman during the time they'd dated, and she'd been a virgin on her wedding night. During the two years they'd been married, she'd never felt that wondrous trembling within her that she'd felt in Joseph's arms. She'd wanted him to make love to her, wanted it very much. "Oh, dear," she said, sighing.

And so, now what?

Could she do it? Could she have a fling while Joseph was in Port Payne, then bid him goodbye with no regrets? Did she have the temperament, the emotional makeup, for an affair? How could *she* know? She'd never been in a position to even consider the possibility before. Cocker spaniel Kendra had lived at home, lived with Jack and lived at home again while finishing her education. She'd been cared for and pampered. And protected from the Joseph Bennetts of the world. Joseph was out of her league. And he was the most exciting man she had ever encountered.

"Well?" Kendra said aloud. "What are you going to do about him, Miss Independent?" Darn it, she wasn't ready to make a decision of this magnitude. She was still charged up over the fact that she'd nearly balanced her checkbook on her own. She had to slow down with regard to Joseph. What she had to do was quit kissing the man! "Fine," she said, nodding decisively. "We're going back to being friendly neighbors until I figure this out. Until I figure *me* out."

Kendra gathered the papers that needed grading and settled at the kitchen table, a red pencil in one hand and a mug of coffee in the other. A glance out the window told her that the day was sunny, bright, and probably cold. Was it too cold for a boat ride on the lake? She'd never been in a rowboat. A yacht, a cruise ship, yes, but never a rowboat. It might be fun—with Joseph.

"Go away, Joseph," she said to the image of him in her mind. "I have papers to grade here."

An hour later a deep frown was on Kendra's face, and she shook her head in dismay. The work turned in by her students was exhibiting no improvement over their initial efforts in September. Except for a few who had obviously given maximum effort to the assignment, her high-school seniors showed little interest in history. They were to have written a three-page report on the man or woman they most admired for contributions to the country, and the choices were far from what Kendra had hoped for.

But it was not only the students' choices of subjects that was bothering her, Kendra realized. She had the niggling feeling that the students were laughing at her, purposely attempting to rattle her by turning in reports on less-than-savory figures in society. It was as though they were daring her to argue the importance of underworld criminals and rock stars.

Most of the students were from low-income families, and Kendra knew that few would be going on to college. They were counting the days until graduation and what they viewed as their chance at new and exciting adventures in the world beyond the confines of high school. Her class was a required course, but it was becoming apparent that most of the students intended to coast through the term and taunt the new teacher in the process.

Kendra sighed and rubbed her now-aching temples. She had to gain control of her pupils. She spent half her time trying to maintain order; the rest of the time she scrambled to keep the students from becoming bored and restless. Why couldn't they see that what had transpired in the past had a tremendous effect on what was happening today? Even more, why couldn't she, the teacher, make them understand?

Leaning against the kitchen counter, Kendra ate a peanut-butter sandwich and drank a glass of milk, her frown still firmly in place. She placed the glass in the sink and was about to start back to the table when she heard a knock at the door.

"Joseph," she muttered, and knew she was cheering up as she hurried to answer the summons.

"Hi," he said, smiling at her after she opened the door. "What did you decide about the boat ride? Want to go? It'll be fun."

"Well, I . . . Sure, why not," she said, matching his smile.

"Great. Bundle up against the cold, and I'll meet you at the dock in a few minutes."

"All right."

In her bedroom, Kendra pulled on red leg warmers and a matching knit hat, then stuffed mittens into the pockets of her pea jacket. She tugged a baggy blue sweatshirt over her pink sweater, poked her arms into the sleeves of her jacket and buttoned it. Rummaging in her drawer, she found a green-and-white striped scarf, which she flung around her neck. Feeling a little embarrassed since Joseph was wearing only jeans, a blue sweater, and a lightweight gray windbreaker, she went out the back door and across the yard to the gate.

The land beyond the row of cabins sloped down to the edge of the lake, one wooden dock servicing each group of four cabins. Joseph was standing next to a rowboat that was nearly devoid of paint. He scrutinized Kendra from head to toe and chuckled.

"Think you'll be warm enough?" he asked.

"I hope so." she said eyeing the boat warily. "Do you think that thing is safe?"

"Sure. Mr. Anderson said it's a first-rate boat. Here, let me fix your scarf. Red and green. You look like a Christmas tree."

"I look like an overstuffed pillow," she grumbled good-naturedly.

But her smile faded as Joseph came close and draped the scarf around her neck, then placed the ends down her back. He seemed to be moving in slow motion as he performed the task, and Kendra felt her cheeks flush.

"Better check your hat," he said, his voice low and husky. "Wouldn't want it to blow off."

Kendra couldn't speak as Joseph tugged gently on the rolled edge of the hat, then slid his hands lower to cradle her face. She stared up at him, their eyes meeting in a heart-stopping gaze.

"Hello, Kendra." His voice made her knees go weak.

And his lips were warm.

He kissed her mouth and gathered her close to his chest as the kiss intensified. Kendra encircled his neck with her arms and stood on tiptoe to fully receive his lips and tongue. She was oblivious to the cold wind and was aware only of Joseph; his taste, his aroma, the strength of his powerful body and the heat that was flowing from him into her.

Joseph lifted his head but did not release his hold on her as he drew an unsteady breath.

"I thought about you," he said, looking directly into her eyes. "Last night, this morning, I couldn't get you off of my mind. I wanted to kiss you, hold you, just like this. Well," he added, smiling, "I will admit that in my daydreams there were a few less clothes between us."

"Joseph, I . . ."

"What are you doing to me, Kendra Smith?" he said. "It's as though you've been with me every minute since you left my cabin last night. You're driving me crazy."

"I am?" she asked. "I guess I should apologize or something."

"No." He pulled her close again, smiling. "You don't need to apologize for being yourself. I've just never met anyone like you."

"You make me sound like a freak," she said into his sweater.

"No way." He tilted her chin up with one finger. "You're a rare, special, unique woman. And, I might add, you're beautiful. Very—" he lowered his head slowly toward hers "—very beautiful."

Joseph brushed his mouth over Kendra's; then his lips melted over hers as his tongue entered her mouth. His kiss quickly became urgent, frenzied, almost rough in its intensity, and Kendra answered it in kind. They drank as though parched, as though they needed each other to assure their next breaths, the next wild beats of their hearts. The sound of their labored breathing was carried away by the wind.

"Boy," Joseph said, jerking his head up. "I start kissing you and...whew!" His voice was gritty as he reluctantly released her and stepped away.

She had promised herself that she wouldn't kiss this man again. But each time he touched her, she dissolved, her good intentions evaporating into thin air. But, oh, the ecstasy of being held tightly in Joseph's arms and feeling his lips on hers.

"Let's go for that boat ride," Joseph offered gruffly.

"Yes" was all Kendra managed to say.

Joseph pushed the boat into the water. "All set," he said, extending his hand to Kendra.

She took a deep breath before placing her hand in Joseph's, then stepped gingerly into the rocking boat. She sat down, and Joseph pushed the boat farther out into the water, then swung himself into it.

"You got your shoes wet," Kendra said, "and the bottom of your jeans. You're going to catch cold."

"Naw, I'm tough. Hot-blooded, remember?"

"How can I forget?" she said under her breath.

The next instant the boat shot forward, and Kendra shrieked.

"What's wrong?" Joseph demanded.

"I'm scared to death, that's what's wrong," she said, clutching the sides of the boat.

"Don't worry about a thing."

"Joseph, are you sure this boat doesn't leak? What if it sinks?"

"Can't you swim?"

"Not in fifteen layers of clothes! I don't think this is a very good idea."

Joseph chuckled. "Trust me. I know exactly what I'm doing."

Yes, he probably did, Kendra thought ruefully. He no doubt always knew what he was doing and why. The type of self-assurance that seemed Joseph's trademark didn't happen overnight. It took years to develop. He knew who and what he was, and where he was going. She envied him that.

Kendra began to relax as she watched Joseph's powerful arms pulling steadily on the wooden oars. The boat seemed to glide through the water as they approached the center of the lake. Then Joseph dragged the oars and the boat came to a stop.

"Perfect," he said. "A patch of bright sunlight. Are you warm enough?"

"Yes, I'm fine."

"We have the whole lake to ourselves."

"Everyone else is home in front of a fire," she said, laughing. "Actually, it's nice out here. Peaceful."

"Yep. You know, you never told me what subject you teach."

"History, to high-school seniors who are very unimpressed by the subject matter."

"I can understand that. They're thinking about graduating, heading for the big time. Who cares what happened a hundred years ago? Bring on the tomorrows."

"Exactly," Kendra said, looking at him in surprise. "That's the attitude I'm fighting with them. How did you know?"

"Because I felt the same way at that age. I saw no purpose in studying old news. I did it—got good grades—because I had long since made up my mind to be a lawyer. But I hated history, calculus, physics. In my opinion, they were wasting my time."

"Most of my students won't be going on to college. They don't have the incentive you did. I'm not reaching them, Joseph. They're still testing me because I'm new; they're bored with what we're studying. I don't know what I'm doing wrong, but I'm beginning to feel I'm gearing up for battle every day. It's very discouraging. The students are... Oh, never mind. I don't want to dump my woes on you. I can't recall ever blithering on like this. My friends say they have to pull information out of me bit by bit. But with you it's like you put a nickel in me and I won't shut up."

"And I listen," he said, his voice low. "I listen because I really want to know who you are, where you're coming from. I'm flattered that you feel comfortable enough to speak freely to me. That's a very nice compliment."

"Oh, well, I—"

"Hey, I know. I'll hunt up my old mirrored sunglasses and visit your school. I'll tell 'em to shape up or I'll turn loose the Bennett brothers. How's that?"

"I don't think the school board would approve," Kendra said, laughing. "Are all your brothers as big as you are?"

"Yeah, except one. Matt has two inches and twenty pounds on me. Every time I see him I tell him he's a terrific guy. He could probably take me out in one punch."

"What does he do for a living?"

"He's a Catholic priest. My mother hollers at him, says with an in like he has, why is it she's still waiting for my babies? Matt just rolls his eyes and glares at me. I really think he's working up to decking me, priest or not." He pulled the oars in, shaking his head.

"And your other brothers and sisters?" Kendra said eagerly. "Tell me all about them, Joseph."

"We Bennetts aren't that interesting."

"Please? I've never known a family like yours."

"Well," Joseph said, shrugging, "the oldest is my sister Angelica."

Kendra listened intently as Joseph recounted tales of his rambunctious family, and she laughed in delight at their antics. He was in partnership, he explained, with his brother David, who was a year younger than Joseph.

"Then David is taking care of things while you're on this vacation?" Kendra asked.

Joseph frowned. "Yeah," he said gruffly.

"Joseph, you never did say why you chose a lakeside vacation at this time of year. Do you come to this area often?"

"I've never been here before. David brings his wife and kids for a couple of weeks each summer. This was his idea, not mine. It's kind of complicated, Kendra." He looked to a spot on the opposite shore. "Say, let's row to the other side and see what's over there."

"Okay," she said absently. Joseph was keeping something from her. He was being evasive about his trip to Port Payne. He'd previously said he was "sort of" on vacation. Why didn't he just tell her what was going on? Of course, it was none of her business, but Kendra had shared a great deal about herself with him. It hurt a little to think Joseph wouldn't confide in her the same way.

Joseph rowed across the lake with lazy, steady motions, then changed direction to skim close to the shore so they could see the type of cabins on the other side. Most were modest structures and seemed to be empty for the winter. They noticed an occasional larger house with smoke curling from the chimney, which indicated that it was occupied by a year-round resident.

"I've really enjoyed this," Joseph said as he started back across the lake. "I didn't know I could sit still for so long. David isn't the idiot I thought he was for telling me to come here. Are you still warm enough, Kendra?"

"Yes," she said, and then, after a moment's hesitation, went on. "Joseph, I'm going to ask this, but you have every right to say it's none of my business. Why did David insist you come to Port Payne?"

Joseph frowned, and his jaw tightened as he pulled the oars with greater force, making the boat shoot forward. Kendra teetered on her seat, then regained her balance.

"Damn, I'm sorry," Joseph said. "Are you all right?"

"Yes, you just startled me a bit."

Joseph dragged the oars in the water, and the boat came to a halt, rocking gently in the chilly breeze. His frown was still firmly in place as he drew a deep breath. He scanned the distant shore as though trying to come to some decision. Finally he leveled his gaze to meet Kendra's.

Seconds passed, and Kendra sat as if pinned in place by Joseph's compelling eyes. She was vaguely aware of the almost musky scent of the lake water, of the lapping sound it made as it licked the boat.

"This is difficult for me," Joseph said quietly. "What I'm concerned about, I guess, is whether or not I can make you understand. Here I am, the guy with the reputation for spieling off great speeches in the courtroom, sitting here fumbling for words."

"You don't owe me any explanations, Joseph. I didn't intend to pry."

"I want you to know, Kendra. I realize that now. You've been so open and honest with me about yourself. That means a great deal to me. As I said before, you're special, rare and beautiful, and I'd be a fool if I didn't recognize it."

"Thank you."

"Kendra, as I've told you, I'm the oldest son in a large family, a close-knit, loving, very old-fashioned family. We were raised to believe that what we did as individuals was a reflection on all of us. The Bennett name was to be respected, protected. As the firstborn boy, I had tremendous responsibilities in regard to the others. I set the pace, the tone, the attitude. We went to a Catholic school, and if a younger Bennett or even one of my two older sisters messed around, the nuns cocked an eyebrow at me, as if to ask what I was going to do about it."

"That hardly seems fair," she commented.

"I never questioned it," he said, shrugging. "That's just the way it was. I gave maximum effort to everything I did, went all out in my studies, in sports and in my role of eldest son. And I've been doing the same thing in my adult life. I simply don't know how to operate other than at full steam ahead."

"Which is why you're such a successful attorney," Kendra guessed.

"I suppose. Can you see the pattern of my life? In charge, in control, the one everybody could count on."

"Yes, it's very clear."

"Last month I had my thirty-sixth birthday and went for my annual check-up. Man, what a shock," he said, shaking his head.

"Joseph," Kendra demanded. "What did the doctor say?"

"Nothing fancy, really. He simply laid it on the line. I either lightened up, quit putting in sixteen-hour workdays, started eating and sleeping properly, or I was heart-attack material. All the warning signs were there in the tests he ran."

"Dear heaven," Kendra whispered.

"I told the doctor to go to hell."

"Joseph, why? You ignored what he said? You didn't slow down? Why?"

"That part's hard to explain," he said, rubbing his fingertips across his forehead. "I didn't know how to handle it, how to deal with the fact that I wasn't performing my duty. It was as though an essential part of me was being stripped away. Joseph Bennett, not big and strong and all things for all people? Hell, no. I was angry, confused, and . . . and scared to death."

"Oh, Joseph." Kendra felt tears stinging her eyes. "I understand. I really do."

Joseph studied her face for a long moment. "Yeah," he said, "I think you do."

"But you're here in Port Payne. You said that it was David's idea. Did you finally tell him what the doctor had said?"

"No. You see," he said, smiling slightly, "the doctor is my brother Rick. I was working late one night. It was about ten o'clock, I guess. I looked up, and in they marched, the brothers Bennett: Matt, Rick, David. Rick had spilled the beans. He told me to sue him if I felt like it, but he wasn't going to stand by and let me kill myself. Man, I was hot. I ranted and raved, called them every name in the book. It suddenly occurred to me that I was outnumbered three to one and that they were getting that mean gleam in their eyes, so I shut up. Then, Kendra, it also hit me that I was very much loved.''

Kendra brushed a tear from her cheek and smiled warmly at Joseph. "Yes, you are. Their coming to see you that night proved how much they love you."

"They're also as rotten as they come," Joseph said, chuckling. "They threatened to tell our mother if I didn't shape up. Believe me, that's enough to give a guy cold chills. Mama Bennett fussing over one of her baby chicks is something to behold. We used to drag ourselves off to school half-dead rather than be subjected to her nursing. I wouldn't have had a moment's peace. I gave up—not gracefully—but I gave up. And here I am, in Port Payne. David made all the arrangements.''

"Wouldn't somewhere warmer have been better?" Kendra asked. "Like the Bahamas or Hawaii?"

"Ah, but then my diabolical brothers couldn't keep tabs on me. Part of the blackmail for not telling our parents is that I can't go home until Rick comes up here and checks me over. I'm supposed to be relaxing, eating, sleeping.''

"Are you supposed to be rowing boats?" Kendra asked, her eyes widening.

"Sure. I can exercise all I want. It's mental stress I'm supposed to avoid, or some such thing. Blood pressure, you know. I told the terrible trio that if I died of boredom it would be on their consciences. You know, Matt told me I'd lost myself over the years, had gotten my priorities all screwed up. I told him to deliver his sermons to his congregation. But then, Kendra, you spoke of being lost, then found, and it struck a nerve. I took a closer look at myself.''

"It can happen to anyone, Joseph," she said gently.

"Yes, but you pulled yourself up and did something about it. It took three big bruisers to force me into action. I refused to face any truths about myself. I couldn't handle it, so I pretended it wasn't there. That's plain stupid. I really hate the idea of discovering a hidden facet of myself at thirty-six. I'm not making any sense, am I?"

"Of course you are. It's frightening to find out you aren't exactly the person you thought you were. I had to say, 'Goodness, I'm not really cut out for this flash-and-dash existence. But who am I, if not who I was?' In your case, you were the leader of the pack, so to speak, the mover and the shaper. But, Joseph, the Bennett children grew up. They love you, but they're leading their own lives. Your clients aren't going to think more highly of you if you keel over in the courtroom from a heart attack. Like it or not, you're human, with strengths and weaknesses. It's time you leaned on others a bit."

"I don't like it."

"You're pouting," she said, smiling.

"Well, hell, the only good thing about this place is the fact that you're here. I couldn't believe it when I opened my door and found you standing on my porch with that baseball bat. My brothers didn't plant you here, did they? You know—a living example of how people can change their lives if they put their mind to it."

"No, it's just a coincidence we ended up as neighbors. I assume Rick said you couldn't pick up where you left off once your tests improve."

"He hollered that great info in my face. He said no man in his right mind kept the pace I had in the past, and those days were kaput. He has a lousy bedside manner, you know. I should be grateful, I suppose, that they care so much.''

"Yes, you're very fortunate," Kendra said quietly.

"You're all alone in your new world, aren't you?"

"I knew it would be that way. It's coming as no surprise to me that my family is thoroughly disgusted by my behavior. But if I had it to do over, I'd still come here. Joseph, your body gave you a warning that you've got to heed and . . . well, I'm sure your brothers said all this. You're going to do it, aren't you? Change the way you lead your life?"

"Yeah, somehow. It isn't going to be that easy, though. But I'll figure it out, I guess. Thanks for listening, Kendra."

"You listened to me, remember? That's what friends are for."

"We're quite a pair," he said, giving her a lopsided grin. "We're each taking our first steps in a new direction. Who knows? We may be able to help each other over some rough spots. Now! I'll row us to shore before you turn into a Popsicle. The temperature is definitely dropping."

"I'm in the mood for hot chocolate. Will you join me?"

"Sold. I never turn down an offer of hot chocolate."

Back on land, Joseph pulled the boat up onto the sloping grass, then, with his arm around Kendra's shoulders, they went into her cabin.

"I'll start a fire while you make the drinks," Joseph said as he took off his jacket.

"Okay, I have to remove a few layers of clothes first," Kendra told him on her way to the bedroom.

"Feel free to take off as much as strikes your fancy." He gave her a comical leer.

Kendra laughed. In her bedroom, she peeled down to her jeans and the pink sweater, then stepped into the bathroom to brush her hair.

How strange it all was, she mused. That two people finding new directions for their lives would end up in such a remote place was uncanny. She could readily understand Joseph's anger and confusion. His body had called a halt to the abuse he was inflicting upon it. In Kendra's case, her mind, her emotions, had rebelled against her way of life. And now they were both starting over, regrouping, reorganizing, reexamining.

Joseph was stubborn, Kendra thought. If he set his mind to it, he could learn to slow down and take better care of himself. He'd find new outlets, relaxing endeavors for his free time. He could, if he so chose, give serious thought to marrying and having the family he yearned for.

Joseph, married? What type of woman would he pick to be his wife? Someone from a large family who would fit in with the boisterous Bennett clan? Would Joseph want a beautiful woman on his arm to perform in the role of the executive's wife, as Jack had done? Well, it made no difference to her who he married. But somehow the thought of a woman in Joseph's life was disturbing to Kendra.

"Don't be silly," she scolded herself, marching from the room. "I don't care who she is."

The fire was crackling as Kendra went into the living room, then on to the kitchen. A short time later she returned with two mugs of hot chocolate, handed one to Joseph, then settled next to him on the sofa

"I'm not sure that fire is going to stay lit," Joseph said. "There're too many ashes in there. It's about a week overdue to be cleaned out."

"Really? I guess I never thought about it."

"Make certain the ashes are completely cool before you . . . On second thought, I'll do it for you tomorrow while you're teaching. You can leave your key with me."

"That's not necessary, Joseph."

"No problem. I have a long day to fill. I'll clean out your fireplace and have a roaring fire waiting for you when you get home. Sound good?"

"Yes," she said, smiling slightly. It sounded heavenly. The thought of Joseph waiting for her in a warm, cozy cabin at the end of a grueling day was absolutely irresistible—but dangerous.

She mustn't become too involved with him, Kendra told herself. It could only lead to heartache. Joseph wouldn't be staying in Port Payne. It probably wouldn't be long before Rick would declare him fit, and he'd leave.

And Kendra would be left there . . . alone.

Four

Delicious," Joseph said, placing their empty mugs on the end table. "You brew a fine cup of hot chocolate."

"I heated up chocolate milk," Kendra said, smiling.

"I promise to keep your recipe a secret," he told her sliding his hand to her nape. "I've filed it in my mind next to my mother's spaghetti sauce."

"I'm honored," she said solemnly.

"You're beautiful." He lowered his head to claim her mouth.

The kiss was long, sensuous and chocolaty. Kendra circled Joseph's neck with her arms and answered the demands of his lips and tongue. He pulled her close, crushing her breasts to his chest as his tongue dipped and dueled with hers. His hands roamed over the soft material of her sweater, then inched up under it to caress her back.

Warm hands, Kendra thought, strong, callused, powerful hands. His touch was ecstasy, but she wanted more!

Joseph lifted his head to draw a ragged breath, then kissed her jaw before moving along her throat. Kendra tilted her head back to receive his magical embrace and the sensations it created within her. His hands moved higher to cup her breasts, his thumbs trailing over the lacy material of her bra. Her nipples grew taut as a moan escaped from her lips. Joseph started to draw the sweater up, then hesitated. Kendra felt him tremble from the force of his restraint. She opened her eyes to gaze into his.

"I just want to see you," he said, his voice raspy.

"Yes," she whispered.

She moved her arms to allow him to remove her sweater, and an instant later her bra followed it onto the floor.

"Kendra," Joseph groaned, then swallowed heavily. "You're the most exquisite woman I've ever seen."

He filled his hands with the weight of her breasts, then dipped his head to draw a nipple deep into his mouth. He suckled gently, rhythmically, as an ever-increasing warmth flowed through Kendra.

"Joseph," she said, clinging to his shoulders.

In a smooth motion, he shifted his weight and hers, bringing her on top of him on the sofa. He gripped her waist to lift her upward. His mouth closed over one throbbing nipple as she wove her fingers through the thick night-darkness of his hair. His hips pressed against her, speaking of his want of her.

And Kendra wanted him.

Desire burned in her, igniting a trail of passionate need as it went. Never had she been filled with such yearning. She was alive as never before, awash with shattering pleasure.

Joseph sought her mouth again. As he thrust his pelvis against hers, a moan rumbled from deep within him. He pressed her mouth hard onto his, one hand on the back of her head, the other on the slope of her jean-clad buttocks. Kendra lay on top of him, feeling his steely muscles and the evidence of his arousal. The kiss deepened. The flames of passion spread like a brushfire.

It was heaven.

It was hell.

It was ecstasy.

But Kendra wanted more.

"Love me, Joseph," she murmured, close to her lips. "Please, Joseph. I want you so much. I've never felt this way before."

Joseph went still beneath her, every muscle in his body seeming to stiffen. In the next instant, he lifted Kendra up and away, depositing her on the end cushion of the sofa as he swung his feet to the floor. He drew in a deep, shuddering breath as he reached for her sweater.

"Cover yourself," he said, his voice a hoarse whisper. He thrust the sweater at her but didn't look at her as he ran his hand through his hair. He rested his elbows on his knees and pressed tightened fists together as he stared into the fire.

"Joseph?" Kendra asked, hearing the shaky tone of her voice. "What's wrong? You look so angry."

He turned to look at her, his dark eyes flashing with an emotion Kendra couldn't decipher.

"Damn it," he snapped, "cover yourself. I'm hanging on by a thread here. Do it!"

With trembling hands, Kendra tugged her sweater on. Joseph was rejecting her. He didn't want to make love with her. She'd never been so bold as to tell a man that she wanted him, wanted to make love with him. Until now—and he was rejecting her. Why? She was a breath away from crying, and she'd never forgive herself if she did. *She would not cry!*

"My brain is mush," Joseph said, frowning as he stared into the fire again. "My body is begging for mercy. I don't appreciate this, Miss Smith. Not one bit."

"You!" she said, scrambling to her knees. "You listen to me, you big lummox. Do I go around offering myself to just any man? No, I do not! Have I ever felt the way I do when you kiss and touch me? No, I have not. And then you reject me? What a rotten thing to do. Oh, you . . ." she said as tears spilled onto her cheeks.

"Reject you!" Joseph said, leaping to his feet and looming over her. Kendra stared up at him, eyes wide. "Is that how you see this?"

"Yes."

"Wrong, Kendra. I was protecting you from me, because I was afraid I'd seduced you into doing something you'd regret."

"How dare you protect me!" she yelled, glaring up at him. "You have no right to protect me." Oh, dear heaven, did that make sense?

"And," he continued, his jaw clenched, "I was protecting me from you."

"What?"

"You said it; I heard you. You've never felt the way you do when I kiss and touch you. Kendra, I won't be a new experience for you in your life as an independent woman, one more thing on your list of adventures, like balancing your checkbook.''

"Huh?''

"Why it matters so much, I have no idea, but it does. No, sir,'' he said, snatching up his jacket, "when we make love it's going to be important, special. I want you. I ache with wanting you, but I'll be damned if I'll be a vacation fling.''

"But—''

"I can't believe I just said all that,'' he muttered, starting toward the door. "I'm slipping over the edge here. I'm losing it, totally losing it.''

"Joseph, I . . .'' Kendra said, spinning around on the sofa.

But the door slammed loudly behind him as he left the cabin. Kendra turned back around, folding her legs Indian-style and crossing her arms over her breasts.

"Well, for Pete's sake,'' she said, frowning. Confusing, terribly confusing. She didn't want Joseph to protect her; she was sick to death of being protected. On the other hand, it was rather dear of him that he'd wanted to be sure he hadn't seduced her into oblivion. But his next tirade? Their lovemaking was to have special meaning, importance? "Fancy that,'' she said, beginning to smile.

Kendra's glance fell on her lacy bra still lying on the floor, and she bent over and snatched it up. She remembered the feel of Joseph's hands and mouth on her breasts, and her cheeks grew warm.

Oh, what ecstasy it had been, she mused dreamily. What wondrous sensations had churned within her. How long she had waited for Joseph Bennett to enter her life. And now he was there, in a world that was hers, created by her. The choices, the decision, were hers to make. And she wanted to be one with Joseph. Yes, their lovemaking should be special and important, and it would have been that night. As filled with desire as she had been, Kendra had known deep within her that to give herself to Joseph would be right and good. He wasn't just a vacation fling. He was Joseph.

And so, now what? The question had returned, taunting Kendra because she still had no answer. Joseph had left angry and frustrated, she realized, and could very well ignore her during the remainder of his stay in Port Payne. Oh, darn, she didn't want him to leave, to walk out of her life as quickly as he'd entered it. She wanted him there, close, laughing with her, talking, sharing and making love with her. He had nudged his way into her solitary world, and she welcomed every rugged inch of him. And he had nudged his way into her heart, her mind, her very soul.

"Darn it, Joseph," she said, "if you don't speak to me again, I'll hire the Bennett brothers to punch you out."

With a sigh, Kendra went into the bedroom to put her bra on and change into a heavier sweatshirt. She should eat dinner, she supposed, then finish grading the papers that were still strewn on the kitchen table.

Once in the kitchen, she realized she hadn't taken any meat out of the freezer. Her first thought was to defrost a steak in the microwave, but then she remembered she didn't have a microwave in the cabin. Uttering a very unladylike word, she fixed scrambled eggs and toast for dinner.

She was returning to the living room after cleaning the kitchen when she heard the sound of Joseph's car starting, then being driven away.

Where was he going? she wondered frantically. There was nothing open in Port Payne on Sunday night. Surely he wasn't driving in to Bay City to see what activities he could find there. He was supposed to be resting, not carousing like an alley cat. The man didn't have the sense he was born with. His health was at stake!

Kendra planted her hands on her hips and narrowed her eyes as the image of Joseph in a smoke-filled bar entered her thoughts. Aha! There would probably be a woman slithering all over him, too, checking him out. His brothers would strangle him if they knew.

And she was worried sick, Kendra thought, plopping down on the sofa. Joseph was in a foul mood because of what had transpired between them. If he'd given her a chance to explain, she would have told him she'd truly wanted him, that he hadn't seduced her past the point of being able to think and that he certainly wasn't an experience even remotely like balancing her checkbook. But he'd gotten his Italian temper all in a snit and stormed out before she could say a word. And now the idiot was probably defying his doctor's orders and zooming off for a hot time in the old town. What a dumbbell.

"Oh," Kendra gasped. The log in the fireplace broke in two and thudded against the grate. The fire flickered, then went out. "Wonderful," she muttered. She didn't know she was supposed to keep the fireplace free of ashes, for Pete's sake. How was a person automatically supposed to know that? It had never occurred to her to check the air in her spare tire, either, and she'd learned about that the hard way, too.

"What else don't I know?" she said to the ceiling. Well, one thing was crystal-clear. Things had changed, she had changed, since she'd met Joseph Bennett. Since she'd been held, kissed and touched by Joseph Bennett. She'd never be the same again because of Joseph Bennett.

The evening seemed to stretch on interminably. Kendra finished grading the papers while part of her listened intently for the sound of Joseph's car. The temperature in the cabin dropped steadily. She turned on the panel ray unit in the bedroom, then shut it off when the room became stifling hot. She hoped some of the heat would remain in the small room. It didn't.

At midnight she peered out the window at Joseph's dark cabin, then with a sigh went to bed, huddling in a ball for warmth. She was cold, her bones ached, and she missed Joseph. She was worried about him. And for two cents she'd shoot him on sight!

The next morning, Kendra was not in a terrific mood. She was stiff from sleeping tightly curled up, her head ached, and the cabin was chilly and damp. She dashed to the window, saw Joseph's car in his driveway and made a face at the BMW. She hurried through her shower and dressed in a gray wool shirt and yellow sweater. The thought of getting into her car and turning the heater on full blast held great appeal, and she settled for a single cup of coffee for breakfast.

As she pulled away, she glanced at Joseph's cabin.

"Don't speak to me," she said to no one. Oh, no, what if he never spoke to her again? Darn it, she hadn't done anything wrong. Homer had been treated more fairly than this, and he'd been guilty of eating the geraniums. She was innocent of any wrongdoing. She'd responded to a man's kiss and touch and he'd thrown a conniption fit. Well, fine. Let him sulk. She didn't care, she told herself, knowing she was lying through her teeth. "Oh, dear," she said. "And oh, damn."

The day went from bad to worse. Kendra's students were even more unruly than usual, and she had difficulty controlling her temper. During lunch, one of the other teachers moaned, "What are we doing in this zoo?" and for the life of her, Kendra didn't know. Her dream of becoming a teacher, her lofty ideals of shaping the minds of the youth of America, were being chipped away by surly teenagers with black leather jackets and multicolor hair.

Kendra took two aspirins for her still aching head and trudged back to her classroom. Through it all, she thought of Joseph.

Driving home in the gathering dusk, she thought of Joseph.

As she parked her car in her driveway and glanced over at his cabin, she thought of Joseph, and sighed. It was a weary sigh, a sad sigh, a sigh that said she'd had a miserable day, her head still hurt, and she might very well treat herself to a long, loud cry.

It wasn't until Kendra was standing on the porch with her key in her hand that she realized that lights were on inside, glowing through the drawn curtains on the windows. She turned the knob tentatively, found the door unlocked and pushed it open.

"Oh," she said softly, seeing the roaring fire in the fireplace. She entered the living room and closed the door behind her.

"Hello, Kendra," Joseph said from across the room.

His voice was low, and as soothing as rich brandy. The sound of it caused a tiny sob to catch in her throat.

"Oh, Joseph," she said, her voice wobbly, her purse and keys falling unheeded to the floor. "I...you... Oh, Joseph."

With long strides he closed the distance between them and pulled her into his arms, holding her tightly as he buried his face in the fragrant cloud of her hair. She leaned against him, wrapping her arms around his waist, inhaling his aroma, relishing his strength and heat, savoring his presence.

And then he kissed her. He kissed her until she went limp in his arms, until her heart was racing and desire swirled unchecked through her. He kissed her with a hunger, an urgency, that engulfed them both. Tongues met, bodies met, and Joseph's arousal pressed hard against her.

With Kendra still in his embrace, Joseph turned and leaned against the door. He spread his legs slightly to nestle her close to his body. Kendra felt as though she were on fire as Joseph's hands roamed over her, igniting a flame of desire as they went. Their breathing was labored as their passions soared.

Joseph lifted his head and drew a ragged breath as he cradled Kendra's face in his hands. She gazed up at him, knowing the message of need evident in his smoky dark eyes was matched by that in her own.

"This," he said, his voice rough, "has been a helluva long day."

"Yes," she whispered.

"I missed you. I wanted to see you, hold you, kiss you, tell you how sorry I was about storming out of here last night."

"I was so worried about you, Joseph. Where did you go?"

"I agreed to play poker with Fred Frazier and his cronies. They play for pennies."

"Oh, thank goodness. I was so afraid you'd gone into Bay City, that you weren't following Rick's instructions. What does Mr. Frazier look like without his fishing hat?"

"He never took it off," he said, smiling. "Come on, let's eat. I've warmed up the spaghetti."

"I'll change my clothes and be right there. Thank you for cleaning my fireplace, for making dinner, for... Joseph, thank you for being here."

"There's no place else I want to be," he said, his voice low. "We have to talk, Kendra. Go change. I'll get dinner on the table."

Kendra nodded and went into the bedroom, leaning against the door for a long moment after she closed it. She drew a deep, steadying breath, aware of the whispers of desire still within her.

They had to talk? she repeated silently while changing into jeans and a green sweater. What did Joseph want to say to her? That they'd met in the wrong place at the wrong time? That it would be best if they stayed away from each other?

"Kendra, are you coming?" Joseph called.

"Yes," she said, opening the door. "Oh, hello, Homer," she added, nearly stepping on the rabbit. "I didn't know you were here."

Homer wiggled his nose and followed Kendra into the kitchen.

"Have a seat," Joseph said, gesturing toward the table. "You really look beat."

"I am," she admitted, sitting down. "This smells delicious."

"The sauce improves with age. Dig in. Did your students give you a hard time today?" he asked, taking a seat opposite her.

"Don't they always? Some of those twerps need a swift kick in the rear end. If only I knew what I was doing wrong."

"You're probably not doing anything wrong. You said yourself that you're teaching a required course to seniors who just want to get the hell out of there. Of course, there's always the possibility that teaching isn't where you belong."

"Don't be silly," she said, "I've always wanted to be a history teacher. When I married Jack he claimed he knew that, but he didn't want me to continue in college. He said there were more important things for me to do...such as attending every important social function in California. My first thought when I divorced him was to get my degree."

"That's fine, but it doesn't necessarily mean it's the right choice for you. My sister Christine always wanted to be a nurse. When she was a kid she practiced wrapping bandages on anyone who'd stand still long enough. One year into nursing school, she knew she couldn't do it. She simply wasn't emotionally equipped to deal with illness, death, all that nursing entails, on a daily basis. There's no shame in admitting you've made the wrong career choice for yourself."

"I haven't made the wrong choice. This is my dream. I'm just very new at it, that's all. I'll figure out how to reach those kids. Somehow."

"Okay," Joseph said gently. "I didn't mean to upset you. It's still early in the school year. Your students will probably settle down, and things will get better."

"I hope so. Enough of that. What did you do all day?" she asked, smiling at him. Keep him talking, she told herself. Then he couldn't zero in on what he wanted to discuss with her. The knot in her stomach was evidence of the fact that she didn't want to hear it.

"Well, I had a real demanding day," Joseph said. "I found Mr. Anderson, convinced him I needed the key to your cabin so I could clean out the fireplace, then I cleaned said fireplace. Later I went into Port Payne and three people asked me if I got your fireplace cleaned."

"That figures," Kendra said, laughing. "That's real fuel for gossip. How decadent of you to have cleaned my fireplace, Joseph Bennett."

"Yep. Then I painted pinecones."

"You what?"

"I wandered into Mrs. Willoby's shop, the one that has all the stuff made out of pinecones. She was painting a whole tableful, and I asked her if I could give it a shot. She's a nice old gal, knows some great dirty jokes. The amazing part was, I thoroughly enjoyed myself. I'm a helluva pinecone painter, too, I'll have you know. If I ever run out of criminals to put on trial, I'll have something to fall back on."

"Do tell." Kendra was laughing softly.

"Sure. But, Kendra? While I was cleaning your fireplace and painting pinecones, I thought about you. I kept looking at the clock, willing time to pass faster so you'd come home to me," he admitted.

Kendra's heart thudded against her ribs as Joseph's voice seemed to drop an octave lower. He was looking directly into her eyes, and she felt pinned in place.

"It was a strange feeling," Joseph went on. "I was functioning, talking, laughing, yet a part of me was concentrating totally on you. When you walked in the door, I felt a sense of completeness. The day in itself had been fine, but when I took you into my arms everything was perfect. The missing link was home."

"Joseph, I—"

"Kendra," he said, covering her hand with his. "I think I'm falling in love with you."

A rushing noise filled Kendra's ears, and she felt as though she couldn't breathe. Joseph thought he was falling in love with her. How wonderful, how frightening. How... She had to respond in some way, say something, something womanly, sophisticated and ultramature.

"Oh" was all that came out of her mouth.

"Oh?" Joseph said, frowning as he slouched back in his chair. "That's it? Just 'Oh'? That's rather deflating, Kendra."

"Oh. Sorry," she added quickly when he glared at her. "I'm stunned, that's all. I guess I expected you to say we shouldn't see each other anymore."

"Why would I say that?"

"Because this isn't realistic. You're only going to be here for a short time. Plus, you're going through major changes in your life, just as I am. You said yourself that our being together mustn't fall into the same category as balancing checkbooks."

"I shouldn't have said that."

"Yes, you should have, because you had a legitimate point. You stomped out of here before I could assure you that I want you, not the experience of having a lover. You didn't seduce me into not knowing what I was doing. I did want you, Joseph."

"Why?"

"What kind of question is that?" she asked, frowning.

"Reasonable. Why did you—do you—want to make love with me?"

"Because I . . . because you . . . Well, for Pete's sake, how should I know? I just do, that's all."

"Could it be, Miss Smith—" he leaned toward her "—that you are falling in love with me at the very moment I'm falling in love with you?"

"You expect me to know?"

"Did you think about me today?" he asked.

"Yes."

"And you said you were worried that I'd disobeyed Rick's orders. You seemed awfully glad to see me when you got here."

"I had a headache," Kendra said, examining her fingernails.

"Which didn't slow you down any when I kissed you."

"Don't be crude."

"I think it's happening, Kendra," Joseph said, staring at the ceiling. "I think this is it, the big time, love in its purest form."

"I don't know what to say."

"Obviously. You've used up a year's supply of 'Oh.' Kendra, I feel like a million bucks. This was fate, don't you see? We were meant to meet in this off-the-wall place. You came clear from California to end up in Port Payne, and I found you. I pushed my body to the limit, and David and company shipped me here. Fate, Kendra."

"But you're going back to Detroit."

"Not yet. We have time to discover everything about each other. We can't walk away from this. Our future happiness depends on us giving this whole thing a chance. The fact that you're still frowning tells me that you have doubts about what's happening between us."

"I don't know what to think. It's all so fast, so confusing."

"Then we'll slow it down, take it nice and easy. I won't rush you, Kendra. I bought some ice cream for dessert. Want some?"

"No. No, thank you," she said absently. Was she in love with Joseph? she asked herself. She didn't know! Did all the new and startling emotions she was feeling add up to love? Shouldn't the realization, the "yes or no," be clear? What if it was true? What if she *did* love him and he loved her? What then? They didn't even live in the same city. She knew nothing of his life-style in Detroit. How close was he to the world she had turned her back on? There were so many questions, so very, very many.

As Joseph sat down at the table and began to devour a huge serving of ice cream, Kendra got up and ran water in the sink.

"*I'll* wash the dishes," he said. "You worked all day."

"But you cooked."

"I heated leftover spaghetti. How's your headache?" he asked, concerned.

"Much better."

"Kendra, come sit down. I said I'd wash those."

"I'll wash; you dry. Eat your ice cream before it melts. Although I don't see how anyone can eat ice cream in the dead of winter."

"This is hardly the dead of winter. Besides, I'm—"

"Yes, I know," she said, laughing, "hot-blooded. A hot-blooded, stubborn Italian."

"That's exactly right." He got up and placed his bowl on the counter, then moved behind Kendra, wrapped his arms beneath her breasts and nuzzled her neck. "You smell good."

"Grab a dish towel," she told him as a shiver ran through her.

"My hands are full." He slid them up to cup her breasts. He pulled her against him, then trailed a ribbon of kisses down the side of her neck as he gently kneaded her breasts. "Heaven itself," he murmured, sighing.

Kendra leaned her head back on his shoulder and closed her eyes as heat flowed through her. As Joseph inched closer, her hold on the edge of the sink tightened.

"Oh, Joseph," she whispered.

"Damn," he said, then gripped her shoulders and moved her away from him.

"What's wrong?" she demanded, turning to look at him.

He snatched the dish towel off the counter and pulled a wet plate roughly from the drainer.

"I said I wouldn't rush you. Slow and easy, remember?"

"I thought that was in regard to knowing if I'm in love with you. That has nothing to do with our making love. I thought you believed me when I told you I want you, not just the experience of taking a lover."

"I do believe you."

"But?"

"You said you were confused by all that's happening. If we make love, it's just going to jumble the picture for you even more."

"You don't know that," she said, her voice rising.

"I can't run the risk! Damn it, Kendra, you're an innocent. For all practical purposes, your marriage doesn't count. I don't want the physical mixed up with the emotional. I want you to get the message that you love me from your heart and mind, *then* your body."

"That's blackmail, Joseph Bennett."

"Men in love do desperate things."

"You don't know you're in love with me," she pointed out, turning back to the sink. "You think you might be, but you aren't sure."

"Yes, I am."

Kendra spun around again to face him, oblivious to the fact that she was dripping soap suds on the floor.

"You sat right there at that table," she said, pointing with a soapy finger, "and told me you thought—"

"And now I know," he interrupted. "I love you, Kendra. I really do love you."

"You're doing your full-steam-ahead routine. That's fine in the courtroom, Joseph, but you can't do that with your emotions."

"Sure, I can," he said, smiling at her. "I already have. I love you. I even like the way it sounds. Joseph Bennett loves Kendra Smith. Fantastic. I've waited thirty-six years to find you. Why play games with it? Facts are facts."

"You're giving me the crazies, Joseph," she said through clenched teeth. "I can't handle this."

"I know, sweetheart," he told her soothingly, then kissed her on the forehead. "That's why I'm doing the slow-and-easy bit for you. You need time to adjust, to get in touch with yourself and discover how much you love me. Without—I repeat, without—the confusion of lovemaking thrown in. Kendra, you're making a real mess of this floor."

"Who?" she asked uncomprehendingly.

"The floor. It's all soapy. We could slip and kill ourselves. I'll wipe it up. Stick your hands back in the sink, will you?"

"Oh, of course." She did as instructed. "My life is out of control," she said to a spoon.

"It is not," Joseph told her from his vantage point on the floor. "A little unsettled, maybe, but not out of control. There," he said, getting to his feet. "All dry."

"Joseph, are you absolutely positive that you love me?" she asked softly, staring into the water.

"Yes, Kendra, I am. I do love you. It hit me fast and hard, right between the eyes. And I'm glad. Hell, I'm ecstatic. Everything is going to be perfect—you'll see. And I won't rush you, I swear it," he said solemnly.

"But you won't make love to me, either."

"No."

"Because you're protecting me, taking care of me, making sure I don't get too confused?"

"Something like that."

"I can't allow you to do that, Joseph," she said, her voice trembling. "I've come too far, fought too hard. I won't turn my life over to you, or anyone. Not ever again."

Five

―――

Hey,'' Joseph said, turning her gently by the shoulders to face him, "I'm not going to control your life."

"Aren't you?" she demanded, tears brimming her eyes.

"No, I—Here." He handed her a towel, then reached behind her to let the water drain from the sink. "I'll put Homer out, then we'll go in the living room and talk."

Kendra dried her hands, tossed the towel onto the counter, then sniffled. Joseph loved her, she told herself. It should be glorious, wonderful—and she'd never been so miserable in her life. He was the man who excited her like none before, who brought a smile to her lips and a warm glow to her heart simply by walking into the room. And she was—

Was she?

Was she in love with him?

Oh, yes, damn it, she was. But she would not, could not, become involved with someone who wanted to control her life, someone who'd try to take away her right to make her own decisions. No. She'd walk away before she'd allow that to happen. But could she walk away from Joseph?

"Oh-h-h," she moaned, then sniffled again.

"Come on," Joseph said, putting his arm around her shoulders.

In the living room, Joseph sat on the sofa, then pulled Kendra by the hand to sit next to him, tucking her close to his side.

"Kendra." He shifted a little, then turned her face toward him. "Look at me. Ah, damn, you're so sad. Love isn't supposed to make you sad. Listen, okay?"

"Yes." She nodded.

"I have no desire to smother you with my love. I respect and admire your independence. I told you that."

"But—"

"Hear me out," he said, raising his hand. "It's because of the changes you made that you're here. And it's because of the changes I was forced to make that I'm also here. For the first time in my life, I've slowed down enough to fall in love. I don't want to blow it by speeding up again, rushing you, expecting you to keep pace with me. I can't lose you, Kendra. I just found you. I'm trying to do this right. I really am."

"Treating me like a child isn't the right way to do it. You're giving me directives about how things should be, then telling me it's for my own good and that you're protecting me."

"Any man worth his salt wants to protect the woman he loves," he said, his jaw tightening slightly.

"Oh, Joseph." She could feel the tears threatening again. "I can't think any more tonight." She circled his neck with her hands. "Kiss me. Please, Joseph, kiss me, hold me tightly. I really don't want to talk any more."

He gathered her in his arms, then brought his mouth down hard onto hers.

Oh, yes, yes, yes, Kendra thought, responding instantly to his kiss. She didn't want to think; she only wanted to feel, savor, to relish, all the wondrous sensations Joseph created within her. She wanted to make love with him. Now.

Kendra slid her hands from Joseph's neck as his mouth continued to ravish hers, their tongues meeting, dueling. She felt the powerful muscles of his chest and let her hand roam lower to inch below his sweater, then up again through the curls of his chest.

"Kendra," he gasped.

"Let me touch you," she begged, her voice hushed. "You touched me, remember?"

"Yeah," he admitted, "I definitely remember, but—"

"And now it's my turn," she said, tugging his sweater upward. "Right?"

"I...um... Right." He frowned but allowed her to draw the sweater over his head and drop it onto the floor.

"Oh, you are so beautiful," Kendra said as she leaned toward him, feathering her tongue over his chest, her fingertips trailing close behind.

Joseph moaned and gripped her shoulders. "This isn't such a hot idea. I'm really in trouble here."

Kendra lifted her hand and slid her tongue along Joseph's bottom lip. His hands shot up, his fingers tangling in her golden hair as he brought her mouth hard on his. He shifted his weight, and Kendra found herself sprawled on top of him. His hands dropped lower to move beneath her sweater, creating a heated flash of passion within her.

Desire crowded Kendra's senses, confusing her, driving her on. She moaned, and Joseph drew the sensuous sound into his mouth. She pushed her hips more firmly against his, and she both heard and felt the groan deep in his chest.

"Love me, Joseph," she whispered close to his lips. "Be one with me."

"Kendra, no," he said, his voice hoarse with passion. "It's too soon. You need time to sort through—"

"I want to make love with you, Joseph, feel you inside me, be yours. Don't you want me, Joseph? Don't you?"

"Damn you, yes!" he said. He swung her around into his arms and was on his feet in the next instant, striding across the room with her as if she weighed no more than a child. His jaw was set in a hard line, and a pulse beat wildly in his neck.

In the bedroom, he set her on her feet, snapped on the small lamp by the bed, then pulled her sweater roughly over her head and tossed it to the floor. An instant later her bra followed it. With trembling hands he unzipped her jeans and shoved them down her slender legs, pushing her shoes off in the process. Naked, Kendra stepped away from the pile of clothes, then looked at him steadily as she stood before him.

He reached for her, then jerked his hands back as though encountering a burning flame.

"What am I doing?" he said, his voice gritty. "This is wrong!"

"No! It's right. I have a voice, Joseph. I'm saying I want you. Don't you understand that? Don't you see me as a woman?"

Joseph's gaze played over her silken skin from head to toe, his breathing rough and labored in the chilly, quiet room. A shadow of pain crossed his features, and he closed his eyes tightly for a moment.

"Please, Joseph," Kendra said in a tiny whisper.

With a strangled moan he reached for her, pulling her to him, taking possession of her mouth in a searing kiss. His hands roamed over her back to cup her buttocks and mold her to him.

Joseph lifted his head, then brought his hands to her breasts, filling his palms, stroking her taut nipples with his thumbs. She ran her fingers lightly over his small nipples.

"Kendra," Joseph gasped.

He turned and threw back the blankets of the bed, then lifted her onto the cool sheets. In jerky motions he shed his shoes and socks, jeans and briefs, then hesitated as he stood by the edge of the bed gazing down at her.

Kendra drank in the sight of him: naked, powerful, bronzed, proportioned as perfectly as a statue chiseled from stone. He was Joseph. And she loved him.

"Joseph," she said, lifting her arms to welcome him into her embrace.

"Say it again," he said, his voice unsteady. "Tell me this is what you want. I can't think clearly anymore. I—"

"Yes. Yes, I want you. Come to me, Joseph. Now. Please."

He stretched out next to her and kissed her again as he caressed the flat plane of her stomach. Kendra sighed with pleasure as desire swirled within her. Joseph had heard her and he had listened. He was there, close, and she knew that soon they would be one. She was filled with immeasurable joy and the flames of passion. She ran her hands over his muscled back and felt him tremble as he tried to restrain himself.

Oh, how she loved this man.

Joseph sought her breasts, and then his hand moved lower. She moaned, writhing under his tantalizing touch.

"Joseph, please."

"Say it," he demanded.

"I want you!"

He moved over her and into her with a thrust that seemed to steal the breath from her body. He slid his arm beneath her hips to bring her closer yet. The rhythm began, deep, thundering. They soared to a place of spiraling senses and nameless yearning. Higher. Closer. Then...

"Joseph! Oh, Joseph!"

"Yes! Hold on to me, Kendra. I..."

He shuddered above her, driving one last time deep within her, his strength passing from him into her. Then he collapsed against her, spent, gasping her name.

Slowly, slowly, Joseph pushed himself up to rest on his arms. She lifted her lashes to gaze into his dark eyes.

"I never knew," she whispered. "It was so beautiful, Joseph, so very beautiful."

He shifted away and rolled onto his back, flinging his arm across his eyes. Kendra frowned and leaned on her arm. She placed his fingertips on his chest, then pulled her hand back as he stiffened at her touch.

"Joseph?"

He didn't respond.

"Joseph, what's wrong? Didn't I please you? Wasn't it good for you?"

"Good?" he said, his voice flat as he slowly lowered his arm. "It was incredible. Yes, it was beautiful, just like you said, but it should never have happened."

"Oh, Joseph, please don't say that. I'm glad we made love. I love you, Joseph."

"Oh, really?" He turned his head to look at her. There was a sarcastic edge to his voice that caused Kendra to shiver slightly. "*Now* you love me," he went on. "Isn't that something. You were all muddled up, but we go to bed together and everything is as clear as a bell. You love me. Hell."

"I do!"

"Right," he said dryly. "Damn it, I knew this would happen. I knew we shouldn't mix the physical with the emotional. I lost control like some kid. You're a helluva seductress when you put your mind to it, Kendra. Did you like turning me inside out? Did it do wonderful things for your newfound independence?"

"No! I—" She couldn't believe what he was saying.

"Well, damn you, lady, you've messed this up royally."

"I love you, Joseph Bennett," she said, her voice rising.

"Quit saying that. I wanted, needed, to hear you say those words before we made love," he said, reaching for his clothes. "Now? Now I don't know what to believe."

"Believe *me*. Believe what I'm saying. Do you think I'm lying to you?"

"No. I'm sure you've convinced yourself that you love me," he said, pulling on his jeans over his briefs. "But you went too fast, didn't think it through, get in touch with yourself. How are you going to separate the emotional from the physical now? It was too much all at once for you. Don't you see? I was trying to protect you... Damn it," he said, raking a hand through his hair.

"I don't want you to protect me!"

"Damn it," he said, gripping her tightly by the upper arms and leaning close to her face. "How can you possibly know what you want? You have no experience at anything."

"Joseph, you're hurting my arms."

Joseph let go of her, then snatched up his sweater and yanked it over his head. He sat down on the edge of the bed to put on his shoes and socks.

"Joseph, please," Kendra begged, placing her hand on his back. "Don't storm out of here angry. It doesn't solve anything."

"I need to be alone," he said, suddenly sounding weary. "I've done things tonight I swore I wouldn't do. I'm not overly fond of myself at the moment, Kendra. I'm going for a walk."

"Joseph, it's dark and cold out there. Can't we talk about this?" She was frantic.

"Not right now," he said, getting to his feet. He turned to look down at her. "I'm sorry. That doesn't cut it, but I *am* sorry."

"Joseph," she moaned, her eyes filling with tears, "you have nothing to be sorry about. We shared something beautiful, special and important, just the way you said it should be. I love you. You've got to believe that."

Joseph looked at her for a long moment, fatigue etched on his handsome features. Then, as a tear slid down Kendra's cheek, he drew a deep, shuddering breath before turning and walking slowly from the room. The sound of the front door closing brought a sob from Kendra's lips.

"Joseph," she whispered as her tears flowed faster. "Oh, Joseph, what have I done to you, to us?"

She sank back against the pillow, pulling the blankets over her chilled body. She'd been wrong, completely wrong. Selfish and self-centered and wrong. In a childish act of defiance, she'd set out to have her own way. She'd used her body to push him over the edge of his self-control to prove how in charge she was of her own destiny. She'd thought only of *her* needs, *her* wants, giving no consideration to Joseph's.

And now, she realized, her declaration of love for him was falling on deaf ears. He had needed, *needed*, to hear her say she loved him before they made love, but she'd ridden roughshod over his senses and done things her way. She was such a fool.

"Why do I have to learn everything the hard way?" she asked aloud, brushing tears from her cheeks. "Why didn't I listen, really listen, to what Joseph was saying to me?" What was he thinking during his solitary walk? she wondered. What conclusions would he come to about them, their relationship? He loved her and she loved him, but she'd made a horrible mistake. "Oh, Joseph," she said, then buried her face in the pillow and surrendered to her tears.

She was a walking rerun, Kendra decided gloomily the next morning. She had another headache, she'd spent a miserable night huddled in a ball and she missed Joseph Bennett. But there were differences in the scenario, too. She was a woman in love, and the soreness of her body gave evidence of the exquisite lovemaking she had shared with the man who had captured her heart.

As Kendra dressed, a rumble of thunder reached her ears, reminding her that she had not yet replaced her broken umbrella. Par for the course, she thought ruefully. Her good intentions to buy another umbrella were behind schedule, and her declaration of love for Joseph Bennett had been late, too. If only she had told him how she felt before they made love.

Kendra dressed in a gray corduroy pantsuit with a black silk blouse. She decided it fit her somber mood perfectly. Outside she shivered, then hurried to her car. There were no signs of life around Joseph's cabin. Kendra sighed, then drove away.

At the school, Kendra avoided the teachers' lounge, where most people gathered for a cup of coffee before the first bell rang. She went directly to her classroom and sat at her desk, staring at the rows of empty desks. She began to think of Joseph, and hot tears burned her eyes. As she blinked them away, Kendra knew it was going to be a long, miserable day.

"Good morning," she said, forcing a smile as two boys entered the room.

"Nothing good about mornings," one muttered. The other grunted in agreement.

Kendra rolled her eyes heavenward and gritted her teeth.

At three o'clock that afternoon, the final bell rang and Kendra's students leaped from their desks. She watched their hasty exit, resisted the urge to stick her tongue out at their retreating backs, then reached for her gradebook to update her attendance records. She wrote a quiz, delivered it to the secretary to have copies made, then reviewed her lesson plan for the next day. At four o'clock she put on her coat and left the building to be greeted by lightly falling snow.

"Snow?" she said, standing on the school steps. "Well, yes, I suppose it is."

With a shrug she headed for her car, unable to resist tilting her head back to feel the unfamiliar gift from nature as it drifted down from the gray sky.

"You're going to bump into something," a voice said.

"Joseph," she gasped, stopping in her tracks.

He was leaning casually against her car, his arms folded loosely over his chest. He wore a sheepskin jacket and the snow dotted his thick, dark hair. Kendra thought he was the most magnificent sight she had ever seen as he pushed himself off the car and approached her.

"What are you doing here?" She was still amazed that he had actually come. "How did you know which high school I taught at? Why are you in Bay City?"

"You're confusing the witness," he said, smiling at her.

Oh-h-h, that smile, Kendra thought wildly. She'd been wondering if he'd ever smile again, if she'd ever see him again. She wanted to rush into his arms and... No, she was going to slow down and think for a change.

"Why are you here?" she asked.

"To see if you'd have dinner with me. I called the board of education, and they told me where you were. I'm in Bay City because you're in Bay City, and I couldn't wait any longer for you to get home. Is there some rule about not kissing teachers in the parking lot?"

"Not in the handbook I read," she said, smiling.

"Come here, Kendra Smith." His voice was husky.

And she went. She went into Joseph's arms with such force that he staggered slightly as he pulled her to his chest. His lips came down hard on hers as she wrapped her arms around his neck. Their tongues met as the lacy snowflakes continued to fall.

"I needed that," he said when he lifted his head. "I love you, Kendra."

"And, I—"

"Let's get out of the cold. Leave your car here. We'll go in mine."

And I love you, Kendra finished in her mind as Joseph assisted her into the car. Had he purposely interrupted her declaration of love, or had he just been concerned about getting out of the cold? Would telling him she loved him set him off on another angry tirade? Where had his thoughts taken him during that long day? Was he now ready to believe that she truly loved him? Oh, dear, her brain was overloaded.

"I called my mother from San Francisco today," Joseph said as he drove out of the parking lot.

"You what? From where?"

"That's where she thinks I am. I'm supposed to be doing some investigative work for an upcoming trial. She wanted to know if everyone had a hot tub, and were there any nice girls there. Oh, and I wasn't to talk to strange men, because she'd heard about those fellas in San Francisco. She's something," he said, chuckling softly.

"Did you speak with any of your brothers?"

"David. He said everything was fine at the office. He settled his case out of court and is reviewing the file on the one I was working on. He's sharp. He can handle it."

"And Rick? Did you speak with him?"

"No. When I went to Port Payne, he said he didn't want to hear my sickly voice for two weeks, then he might consider chatting after that. He's a dud."

"How are you feeling, Joseph?"

"Fine. I never did feel sick. I realize now that I was very tired, but I've caught up on my sleep. I'll have to take Rick's word for it that I need this much time off. He claims he's a brilliant doctor."

"I'm sure he is. I have a feeling that all you Bennetts give maximum effort to everything you do."

"Like screaming and hollering?" he asked, glancing at her and smiling.

"That, too," she said, laughing softly.

"Kendra," Joseph began, frowning suddenly, "there are a hundred things I need to say to you about last night. I paced across my living room so many times today that Homer finally got fed up and hid out in the bathroom. Look, we'll talk, get it all squared away, work it through. Bottom line is that I love you very much."

Kendra took a deep breath. "And I love you, Joseph," she said, looking at him anxiously.

"Here's the restaurant. How does a thick, juicy steak sound?"

"Fine," she said, although she felt a sudden flash of anger. So, that was how Joseph was going to play it. He'd totally ignored her declaration of love. That was better, she supposed, than his yelling in her face, but for Pete's sake, this was ridiculous. She loved him!

The maître d' led them to a cozy table with a candle flickering in the center. Joseph removed his jacket to reveal a red V-neck sweater over a white open-necked shirt. Kendra was nearly mesmerized by the fascinating play of the candlelight over his rugged features and his thick dark hair. Then she vaguely registered the fact that Joseph was speaking to her.

"Pardon me?" she said.

"Where were you?"

"Looking at you."

Before Joseph could reply, the waiter appeared to take their order of steak, baked potatoes and salad. Kendra declined the offer of wine.

"Not if I'm driving home in snow," she said. "I've never done that before, and I'll need all my wits about me."

"It isn't sticking, but we'll have some wine the next time."

The waiter nodded and moved away.

"Kendra," Joseph said, "before we hit on the heavy-duty stuff about you and me, there's something else I have to discuss with you."

"Which is?"

"I talked to Mr. Anderson today."

"Is there something wrong with your cabin?"

"No. It's fine, such as it is. Drafty as hell, but... Anyway, the problem is the roads. There's no snow-plow in Port Payne. When the first heavy snowfall comes, you won't be able to get out of the driveway."

"What?" she asked, her eyes widening.

"Anderson just stood there with a blank expression on his face. He honestly didn't think of it when he rented you the cabin."

"But I have to get out. I have to teach every day. Good grief, what am I going to do?"

Joseph leaned back in his chair and crossed his arms, a slight frown on his face as he looked at her. Kendra waited, but he didn't speak.

"Did you fall asleep?" she finally said, leaning toward him.

"No, I'm trying to avoid trouble. If I tell you what I think you should do, what will happen? Will you thank me for taking the time to sort it through? Or will you accuse me of trying to tell you what to do and control your life?"

"Oh, Joseph, don't," she said, sighing. "Can't we just discuss the snow for now?"

"Yeah, okay." He matched her sigh as he rested his arms on the table. "The way I see it, there's only one solution."

"Move here to Bay City," she said, frowning.

"Yep. And as soon as possible. Anderson said the first big snowfall could come anytime. He felt bad about the whole thing and said he'd refund your rent money."

"I see," Kendra said quietly. "I guess I should try to find a place this weekend. But then I'll be here, and you'll be there, and—"

"That's next on the agenda," Joseph interrupted. "I don't know when Rick is going to give me the okay to go back to work. So here it is, Kendra, pure and simple. I want to move to Bay City with you and share an apartment and a bed for as long as I'm able to stay here. Well?"

Kendra's heart leaped. Now that was more like it. Oh, what ecstasy to wake up in the morning nestled close to Joseph after a night of making love. It was wonderful. But it was...temporary, short-term. No, she wouldn't think about that part now.

"Kendra?"

"Yes," she said, smiling, "that sounds perfect."

"Are you sure?"

"Positive," she said decisively.

"Really?"

"Joseph, yes."

"Would you like to think it over?"

"No. It's settled."

"Only if you're sure."

"I've made my decision," she said, smiling at him warmly. "You didn't railroad me into this."

"Good. Great, in fact. Top-notch," he said, nodding.

"Joseph, I'm going to confess something."

"Oh?"

"I hate that cabin. I'm so tired of being either too hot or too cold. There is nothing character-building about cleaning out grungy fireplaces. Defrosting the refrigerator every other week is the pits, and I want to wiggle my toes in thick-piled carpeting."

"I'll be damned," Joseph said, laughing. "I'm amazed you admitted all that."

"Why? Because Port Payne was part of my statement of independence? I enjoyed the peacefulness at first, but I've grown past that now. Abraham Lincoln might have thought that cabin is ritzy, but I think it's awful. I wasn't cut out to be a pioneer. Call me pampered, but I like to have hot water during my entire shower."

Joseph whooped with laughter, then moved back to allow the waiter to place their meals in front of them.

"Steak," Joseph said. "I've definitely had my fill of spaghetti for the time being. If my mother heard me say that, she'd light another candle for me."

They ate in silence for several minutes, thoroughly enjoying their food.

"I'm glad you won't be making that drive to Port Payne twice a day," Joseph said finally. "That's an empty stretch of road for a woman alone."

"The scenery is lovely."

"Yeah, well, if your car broke down you'd be stranded, or at the mercy of any weirdo that happened along. Your moving to Port Payne in the first place wasn't a terrific idea, but at least you're getting out of there."

"It *was* a good idea at the time, Joseph. It was exactly what I needed. I'm not sorry I went there."

"Whatever," he said, shrugging.

"I didn't do it on a whim."

"Okay. How's your steak?"

"Darn it, Joseph, my decision to live in Port Payne was right for me when I first arrived." She had to make him understand.

"Kendra, what are you getting so uptight about? You don't have to justify your actions. I didn't even know you then."

"Oh? You mean I only have to justify my actions starting with the day I met you?"

"Ah, man, you're pushing. What's with you? You seem determined to pick a fight with me. It takes two to argue, and I'm bowing out of this dance, kid. Eat your dinner."

"Oh, Joseph, I'm sorry. I'm being terribly defensive. I've had a letter a week from my mother telling me how foolish my actions are. She'll gloat when I tell her I've moved to Bay City, then she'll assume my next step will be to go back to California. I didn't mean to take it out on you."

"That's okay," he said, smiling. "I have broad shoulders."

"You have marvelous shoulders."

"Oh, yeah? he said, laughing. "Anything else pass muster?"

"I'm sure you've heard it all before, Mr. Bennett. The women in your past were not blind."

"Women? What women?" He made his face look innocent.

"Spare me. In the Old West, you would have been known as a lusty buck."

"Oh, good grief," Joseph said, dissolving in a fit of laughter.

Kendra's laughter instantly mingled with Joseph's. He took her hand in his and held it tightly.

"There it is," he said, smiling, "the sunshine sound. Oh, Kendra, I love it when you laugh. We've got so much going for us."

"We have problems, too," she pointed out softly.

"I know, but anything worth having is worth maximum effort. We'll slow things down and figure everything out."

"Are you still sorry we made love?" she asked a little anxiously.

"It's pretty tough to regret something that beautiful, but I still don't like the idea that I lost control. I couldn't have stopped if I'd had a gun put to my head."

"I didn't want you to stop. It wasn't your fault. I think I seduced you."

"I *know* you did," he said, shaking his head. "That blows my mind. I'm used to being in charge of those types of situations."

"Aha! Your macho image received a lethal blow."

"It was shot straight to hell, that's what it was. Tonight, Miss Smith, we make love by mutual consent. How's that?"

"Lovely," she said, smiling warmly.

Joseph cleared his throat. "This entire conversation is rather rough on my libido. I'm changing the subject. I have a plan."

"Oh?"

"You leave your car at the school and ride home with me. I'll drive you back in the morning and spend the day looking for apartments. You give me your general price range, and I'll try to make arrangements to have you check them out when you're finished for the day."

"Well, I... That's a lot of trudging around for you."

"Beats painting pinecones again. Besides, there're things I want to be sure of: the general caliber of the neighborhood, quality of locks on the doors and windows, whether there's a security guard, lighted parking lots, all kinds of things. You might get suckered in by central heating and thick carpeting."

"Oh, thanks," she said, frowning. Lighted parking lots? she repeated silently. She never would've thought to check on such a thing. Well, what could one expect from a person who didn't have enough sense to buy a new umbrella and from a woman who picked the worst time possible to tell her lover that she loved him? Oh, darn, when—*when*—was she going to be all grown up and doing fine?

Six

———

The snow was still falling lightly when Kendra and Joseph emerged from the restaurant, but it melted as soon as it hit the ground. Joseph drove the BMW over the wet roads with the ease of one accustomed to driving in inclement weather. Dreamy music drifted through the air from the radio, and Kendra leaned her head back, closed her eyes and sighed with contentment.

How heavenly it all was, she mused. She and Joseph were driving home together. Then, in a cabin warmed by a blazing fire, they would make love. The move to Bay City meant more changes in her life, but she and Joseph were going together. He would be there to—

Kendra opened her eyes and glanced quickly at Joseph as he concentrated on his driving. To protect and care for her, she thought, watch over her and make decisions for her. No! She wanted—*needed*—to be an equal partner in their relationship, not a child under the wing of a guardian angel.

She was leaving her crummy little cabin because Joseph had discovered the hazards of the coming winter. He thought that her living in Port Payne had been foolish in the first place, and now he was seeing that she moved into Bay City, to an apartment she would select from an approved list furnished by him.

It was all so confusing. Joseph had had the foresight she'd lacked and had checked with Mr. Anderson about the availability of a snowplow. She was to be spared the horrifying experience of finding herself snowbound in her cabin, a cabin she had admitted was rapidly losing its charm.

And Joseph knew the ins and outs of apartment-hunting, while she did not. His knowledge would keep her from moving into a place that was wrong for her.

But he was doing it all for her. She felt like a cocker spaniel again. No, this time she was a white rabbit, being taken care of by Joseph just as Homer was.

Kendra wanted to rant and rave, stamp her foot, demand that Joseph back off and allow her to make her own decisions. But she'd only sound like a total idiot, she thought miserably. She would stand there and declare she was moving to Bay City before she got snowbound, then count off on her fingers the security features she'd look for in her new apartment. She'd simply be repeating every conclusion Joseph had come to. He'd decide she was a raving lunatic.

No, Kendra realized, Joseph had done nothing wrong. Yet she had an uneasy feeling in the pit of her stomach, a vague sensation of dread, of wariness. She had to hold fast to...to herself, defend the woman who was emerging from the cocoon she'd lived in. She mustn't lose herself again.

Kendra sighed.

"Tired?" Joseph asked, glancing at her.

"What? Oh, no, I'm fine. I hope Libby comes to Port Payne before I move so I can say goodbye to her. Actually, I'd like to see everyone. They've all been so nice to me."

"We'll put it on the agenda. They'll have enough gossip for the winter when they find out we're moving to Bay City together."

"That's true," Kendra said. "We'll have performed an important civic service by alleviating some of their boredom."

Joseph chuckled, then a few minutes later turned into the driveway at Kendra's cabin.

"Home," he said. "Our castle awaits."

"Cold castle."

Inside the cabin, Joseph lit a fire, then said he would go retrieve Homer from his backyard.

"I'd better shower at my place, too," he added. "There isn't enough hot water for us both or room in that dinky thing to shower together. I shall return."

"All right."

"Kiss me goodbye," he said, pulling her into his arms.

The kiss was long, powerful and sensuous, and Kendra's knees were trembling when Joseph released her and left the cabin.

"Potent stuff," she said, pressing her hands to her flushed cheeks.

In the chilly bedroom, Kendra quickly shed her clothing, then dashed into the bathroom to stand under the shower. A tingle of excitement over what was soon to take place between her and Joseph caused her to smile as the steamy water gave her skin a peachy glow. She dried with a fluffy towel, then slipped on her cranberry-colored velour robe. After brushing her hair, she left the bathroom with every intention of hurrying into the living room to stand in front of the fire.

"Oh," she gasped in surprise. "I didn't expect you back so soon, Joseph." He was kneeling in front of the panel ray unit on the wall, having removed the front section.

"I don't have any more hot water than you do. Calls for speedy showers."

"What are you doing?"

"Adjusting the temperature of this unit so we don't cook. I did it to mine. It's very high-tech knowledge, you understand. I turned about three screws with a quarter. There," he said, replacing the front panel. "All set."

Kendra stared at the panel ray unit as though she'd never seen it before in her life. Joseph took a quarter out of his pocket and fixed it? she thought, incredulous. She'd been freezing to death rather than roast, and he just calmly steps up and fixes the dumb thing?

"How did you know what to do to that?" she asked.

"I just looked it over and figured it out." He was dressed in jeans and a shirt that was unbuttoned and hung free of his pants. "That's a much better temperature, don't you think?"

"Yes, it's perfect. It never occurred to me that I had any choice but to fry or freeze."

"Life is full of choices, my sweet," he said, moving to her and drawing her into his arms. "The fact that we're both in Port Payne is proof of that."

"You were blackmailed into coming," she said, smiling up at him.

"Technicality. I'm here."

"And I'm glad," she said, sliding her hands up his chest.

Joseph lowered his head to kiss her throat and then her mouth, his tongue delving deep within. As the kiss intensified, he pushed Kendra's robe off her shoulders. She moved her arms and the velour dropped to the floor.

"Lovely," he murmured, staring hungrily at her. Then he claimed her mouth again.

Even as he kissed her, Kendra removed his shirt, then sought the snap on his jeans. She was awash with desire, trembling in his grasp. She wanted him—all of him—now.

He swung her into his arms and kissed her deeply before moving to the edge of the bed. He set her on her feet, threw back the blankets, then lifted her onto the cool sheets. After shedding his jeans and briefs, he stretched out next to her, not touching her, only looking at her. The heat of his gaze inflamed her body, and she reached for him.

"I love you, Joseph," she whispered. "I want you, and I love you."

He hesitated a moment, then his mouth came down hard on hers. His roaming hand became an instrument of pleasure, of sweet torture, as it moved over her. Then his lips followed the trail his hand had blazed, igniting her passion even further.

"Joseph," she gasped.

"Soon," he said, his voice gritty. "Soon, Kendra."

His mouth found her breasts, giving loving attention to first one, then the other, as he drew the taut nipple

into his mouth. Kendra sank her fingers into his thick
hair, savoring the sensations rocketing within her until
she could bear no more.

"Oh, Joseph, please," she said, nearly sobbing.

He entered her slowly, filling her with his masculinity, sheathing himself in the velvety darkness of her
welcoming femininity. Kendra lifted her hips to meet
him, to receive all of him, to take him unto herself.

The rhythm began. Joseph held back, keeping the
pace gentle, almost teasing, as Kendra gripped his
shoulders. She burned with the need of him, ached with
the want of him. She arched her back and Joseph
groaned deeply, driving hard within her.

"Is this what you want?" he demanded.

"Yes. Oh, yes!"

"I love you, Kendra."

They went on the promised journey to the place of
hazy sounds and swirling colors. They teetered on the
edge, then slipped over, going past reality to an unknown shore. They called to each other, clung to each
other, as the spasms coursed through them. And then
they drifted back, slowly, gently, sated.

Joseph kissed Kendra, then eased away, reaching for
the blankets to cover them. She snuggled close to his
side, and he ran his fingers through her silky hair.

"Incredible," he said. "Making love with you is not
really describable."

"I feel the same way, Joseph. I think maybe part of
it is because we're in love with each other."

"Kendra, look, you—"

"No, it's my turn to be listened to. You said that life
is full of choices. I'm just beginning to learn how to
make them. Some will be wrong; others will be very
right. I love you, Joseph. I've chosen to recognize and

embrace that love, give it space in my life and nurture it. But how will that love grow if you don't believe in it? You've got to trust in me enough to know I truly love you. I won't say those words again until you do believe me, because it hurts too much when you ignore them. I've done all I can to convince you that I'm sincere."

A silence fell over the room, broken only by the hum of the wall heater. The bedside lamp cast a rosy glow, but Kendra did not tilt her head back to see the expression on Joseph's face. She spread her hand flat on his chest, feeling the steady beat of his heart beneath her palm as the seconds turned into minutes.

Kendra mentally begged him to believe her, to believe in her love for him. She waited, her heart pounding.

"Kendra," Joseph said finally, his voice low, "I think I'm a very lucky man to have your love. I'm honored. I love you. You love me. Nothing can stop us now."

"Oh, Joseph," she said, looking up at him as tears spilled onto her cheeks.

"Say the words for me, Kendra. It will be as though I'm hearing them for the first time."

"I...love...you. I love you, I love you, I love you," she said, smiling through her tears.

"Do you forgive me for being so stubborn about it?"

"Yes."

"Then I'd say we've got it made." He covered her mouth with his.

It was much, much later before they slept.

The next morning, Kendra slipped out of bed as quietly as possible. She had awakened even before the alarm rang and shut it off before it could disturb Joseph. Then she spent a full ten minutes simply gazing at him as he slept. He lay on his back. His hair was tousled, his beard rough and dark. To Kendra, he was beautiful. She wanted desperately to tangle her fingers in the dark curls on his chest. Even in peaceful slumber he seemed to touch her with his power and masculinity.

And Joseph believed in her love.

It was glorious. Life was glorious. Even the gray, gloomy weather was glorious, and Kendra hummed softly as she showered and dressed, then made coffee. Minutes later she brought a steaming mug to Joseph and sat on the edge of the bed.

"Joseph?" she said. "Wake up."

"Mmm," he mumbled, not opening his eyes.

"Rise and shine. I can't be late for school. I brought you some coffee."

"Okay," he muttered, then yawned as he opened his eyes. "You look nice, really sharp."

"Thank you," she said, glancing down at her rose-colored wool dress. "Sit up and drink this."

The blankets dropped lower as Joseph pushed himself against the headboard, and Kendra's hand was trembling slightly as she gave him the mug. Their gaze met and held for a long moment.

"Don't look at me like that," Joseph finally said, "or I'm going to haul you back into this bed."

"That sounds wonderful, but impossible. I have to go shape the minds of today's youth."

"How are your little demons?"

"Still rowdy and bored. We're almost at the end of the first grading period, and the majority are failing. They've got to buckle down, or they're not going to graduate."

"Choices, remember? They know they're not studying. They've made that decision."

"But maybe it's me, the way I'm teaching."

"Nope, I can't buy that," Joseph said. "Well, move your gorgeous tush so I can get myself in gear. I'll pull on my jeans, grab my rabbit, go home and shower, shave and dress. You could, of course, kiss me before I go."

"My pleasure, Bennett."

"Then do it, Smith."

The kiss was long and powerful, and Kendra wondered if her legs were going to support her when she finally moved off the bed.

Joseph returned, dressed, in record time. They headed for Bay City.

"Wish me luck," Joseph said in the parking lot of the school. "I have no idea what the apartment situation is. When should I pick you up?"

"Make it four-thirty. That'll give me time to get through my paperwork after the last class leaves."

"Got it," he said, leaning toward her. "Have a good day." He kissed her quickly. "I love you."

"I love you, too," she said, smiling, then opened the door.

Kendra stood and waved goodbye as Joseph drove out of the parking lot.

"Mercy, what a hunk of stuff," a voice said.

Kendra spun around. "Oh, hi, Ruth."

"Kendra, you've been keeping secrets from me," her colleague said as the two walked toward the building. "What's his name?"

"Joseph Bennett."

"Is he going to take you away from this madness? Would he take me, too? I swear, I can't handle this much longer. This is my fourth year of teaching, and I'm burning out fast. How are you doing?"

"Not terrific," Kendra said, frowning. "I feel like a warden, not a teacher."

"Isn't that the truth? You know, Kendra, as a math teacher, I have skills that are marketable in private enterprise. I'm seriously considering not renewing my contract here next year. How about you?"

"I want to teach, Ruth. It's always been my dream. I just didn't think it was going to be like this. I'm really very discouraged."

"So grab your hunk of stuff and ride off into the sunset."

"And be what? A decoration on his arm? No, I need to be a teacher and know I'm accomplishing something on my own."

"No offense, Kendra, but I don't think you're cut out for this. You could use your education in another area."

"No," Kendra said firmly, "I'm a teacher."

"We'll see," Ruth said quietly.

Kendra was frowning as she entered her classroom, still thinking about her conversation with Ruth. Ruth was wrong. Kendra *was* meant to be a teacher, and she'd be a good one once she had more experience. This was her dream, her... No, she admitted to herself, what she faced each day in that classroom was not at all the way she'd dreamed it would be. But she couldn't give up. She needed desperately to succeed in the career she'd struggled so hard for. Things would get better. They just had to.

Kendra pushed aside her distressing thoughts and greeted the students as they entered the room. She couldn't help thinking about Joseph and wondering if he would have a variety of apartments to show her by the end of the day. She didn't allow herself to dwell on the fact that Joseph's stay in Bay City was going to be miserably short. They loved each other and would somehow find a way to be together as much as possible. They'd choose a place to live, then close the door on the world.

"Just Joseph and me," Kendra said under her breath during her last class. "Oh, yes, and Homer."

"Homer?" a student said. "Abraham Lincoln's wife's name was Homer?"

"I'm sorry," Kendra said, laughing. "I didn't hear your question."

"Homer who?" a girl asked.

"He's a rabbit," Kendra said.

"I'd rather have a dog," a burly youth said. "Not some dumb rabbit. Dogs can be trained for stuff like sniffing out drugs and bombs."

"My uncle is a cop," another interjected. "He takes one of those dogs in his patrol car. They're smart dudes, those dogs."

"I saw a special on TV about that," a girl said. "They showed German shepherds that could . . ."

Kendra sank onto her chair, absently telling herself to close her mouth, which had dropped open. The interchange among the students became boisterous as more and more entered into the lively discussion about the use of dogs in law-enforcement agencies. Kendra had never seen her pupils so animated and enthusiastic.

"Dobermans," one said. "Now, there is a dog. You give every soldier in the army a Doberman, and there's no country nowhere gonna mess with Americans."

"That's not practical," a girl said. "You'd increase the defense budget, having to feed and train them."

"The soldiers?"

"No, stupid, the dogs."

This was wonderful, Kendra thought, her eyes dancing with excitement. They were thinking, really thinking, and sharing, and... Oh, good grief, they were supposed to be studying Abraham Lincoln. Was she wrong to allow this discussion to go on? What was she to do? She was just sitting there like a lump.

"Poodles!" a boy exclaimed, jumping to his feet. "In the army? Are you nuts? I bet you'd put bows on their heads."

The bell rang. The students filed out, a half dozen still engaged in the debate. Poodles were extremely intelligent, a girl said, and three boys snorted in disgust.

"I forgot to give them their homework assignment," Kendra said to the empty room. Had she just witnessed a disaster? Had she totally lost control of her class, or was healthy, animated debate worthwhile even if it wasn't on the proper subject matter?

Kendra sat staring into space for a long moment, then shook her head in defeat, absolutely confused.

"Joseph," she said, shifting mental gears. "Oh, I hope he found some apartments we can look at."

Kendra opened a file and quickly scanned the next day's lesson plan. She'd managed to post the attendance in her gradebook during the day and had only the last class to do. She'd just completed the task and snapped the book closed when the sound of a deep voice caused her to jump in her chair.

"May I come in even if I don't have an apple for the teacher?"

"Joseph!" she said, getting to her feet. She hurried toward him. "How did you know where I was?"

"I worked some Bennett charm on the secretary up front," he said, smiling as he pulled her into his arms.

"Oh, no you don't." She wiggled free. "There are still students straggling along out in the hall."

"Well, damn," he said, grinning. "Where's your sense of daring?"

"It's not in this room, that's for sure."

"So, this is the torture chamber, huh?" he said, glancing around. "School hasn't changed that much since I went. There're still scarred-up desks and grimy windows. How did the little darlings treat you today?"

"The last class got into a marvelous debate. Thing is," she said, frowning, "it wasn't remotely close to the subject we were studying. I still don't know if I made a mistake in letting them go on and on. There are no rules for this type of thing. Nothing I learned in college prepared me for... Enough of this. Did you find some apartments?"

"Let me ask you something. You like history, right? Studying what has gone before, digging up old facts?"

"Yes, of course."

"It's the teaching part that is bursting your bubble. In other words, your love of history is still intact."

"I didn't realize it would be such a battle to get the students to want to learn. I was naive enough to think they'd be as excited about history as I am. What a joke. Why?"

"Just thinking," Joseph said, tapping his temple with his fingertip. "I'll clue you in later."

"Whatever. What about the apartments?"

"Are you finished here?"

"Yes, I'm ready to leave."

"Let's go," he said, striding toward the door.

Kendra snatched up her purse and coat and hurried after him.

Outside, Joseph assisted Kendra into the car, then walked around to slide behind the wheel. Instead of turning the key in the ignition, he pulled her into his arms and kissed her until Kendra's heart was racing.

"I want you," Joseph said. "You're in my mind all the time. Then when I see you and take you into my arms, I ache with wanting you. I think about being inside you, and I go crazy. I... Damn, tell me to talk about apartments."

"Talk about apartments," Kendra said breathlessly, desire churning within her.

"Right." He pushed her gently away from him. "Apartments."

"And?"

"Kendra," he said, frowning, "the rental situation here is grim. None of the houses listed in the paper were right for you, and the apartments...well..."

"Well?" she prompted.

"I checked out the ones advertised and rejected them flat. Then I saw a realtor. He confirmed my suspicions that pickings are slim, but he did know of one place that was available. He took me to see it."

"And?"

"It's nice, very sharp, passed everything on my mental list, including thick brown carpeting for you to wiggle your cute toes in. It's furnished, has a security monitor, is on the fourth floor of a fairly new building, has—"

"Joseph, I'm getting excited," she said, her eyes sparkling. "Can we go see it now?"

"Well, yeah," he said slowly, "we can see it now, and tomorrow, and whenever we want."

"Pardon me?"

"I rented it."

"You—you what?" she asked, her eyes widening.

"I didn't want to run the risk of it being snatched up by the time I could get you back over there."

"You rented an apartment for me that I haven't even seen?" Kendra said, her voice rising. "How could you do such a thing?"

"With my checkbook," he said, grinning at her.

"This isn't funny, Joseph."

"Look, you'll love it. Let's drive over there, okay? Kendra, I had to act fast or lose the place. If you'd calm down, you'd realize I had no choice but to go ahead. I put everything in my name and—"

"What!"

"It was easier that way. I have great credit in Detroit. The utility companies just phoned down there and checked me out. Everything is ready to roll," he said, turning the key in the ignition. "Including your temper, apparently. You've got your lips stuck together like you just ate a lemon. Would you stop and think for a minute here? That apartment would probably have been gone by now. I had to act fast."

Kendra slouched back against the seat, folded her arms over her breasts and scowled. She didn't like this one little bit. When she and Jack had returned from their honeymoon, he'd handed her a key to an enormous house that had been completely furnished by a decorator. She'd had no voice in where she lived, no voice in anything. Now it was happening all over again. Joseph had no right to have rented that apartment without her knowledge.

But what would she do if he hadn't done it? she asked herself. She had to leave Port Payne before the first heavy snowstorm. It was rather tough to move to a new city when you didn't have a place to live. And that was exactly what would happen if she threw a tantrum and refused to accept the apartment. Somehow, Joseph had managed to be right again, and one step ahead of her. She had a sneaky suspicion that the apartment was going to be perfect, the rat.

And it was. The rooms were large and nicely decorated in earth tones, the kitchen bright and cheerful. There was one bedroom, a living room, kitchen and small eating area. The bathroom had both a tub and shower. The carpeting was thick and inviting, and all the rooms were well heated.

Kendra wandered through the apartment while Joseph leaned casually against the wall by the door.

It was really lovely, Kendra admitted to herself, everything she could have hoped for. She wanted to rush into Joseph's arms and tell him she adored it, that she could hardly wait for the two of them to move in. But a part of her was numbed by fear, by a feeling of dread that she was once again losing control of her life. She felt torn in two.

"So," Joseph said, "what do you think?"

Kendra turned to face him. "It's very nice," she said quietly.

"Nice enough to manage a smile?"

"Oh, Joseph," she said, sighing, "I must seem very ungrateful for all you did today. It's just that—"

"I know," he interrupted her. "I took over decisions that were yours to make. But don't you understand that I had no choice?"

"Yes, a part of me knows that."

"Well, is there a part of you that would like to go for a hamburger? Then we could drive to Port Payne and collect enough of our stuff to spend the night here."

"Fine."

"Kendra, could you lighten up?" Joseph said. "I realize this whole thing isn't setting well with you, but the fact that I understand how you feel should be worth something. I did this *for* you, not *to* you. Independence is great, but not when you push it past the point of making sense. I knew you'd like this place. If I'd held off so you could make the decision yourself, it wouldn't be ours now."

"I know you're right. We seem to reach the same conclusions about things, but I wish I could be the first one there once in a while. It's so hard to explain. You've done nothing wrong, Joseph. I realize that. But by the same token, I haven't done anything right. Or, closer to the truth, I haven't done anything!"

He crossed the room and pulled her into his arms. "Hey, it would be different if I were trying to shove an apartment at you that you hate, but you *like* this place. We love each other, Kendra. Does it really matter so much who made what decision, as long as we're both pleased? Tell you what. You pick where we eat dinner. Any fast-food joint in town, so we can be on our way to Port Payne. What'll it be? Greasy hamburgers? Greasier chicken? What?"

"Oh, Joseph," she said, smiling, "you have a way of forcing me to realize I'm acting silly."

"That's not my intention."

"I know. I'm delighted with this place. It's perfect, and I thank you. I do appreciate all you did today."

"Show me," he said, waggling his eyebrows.

"My pleasure."

The kiss was long and passionate, and Kendra responded instantly to the demands of Joseph's lips and tongue. She welcomed the desire that swirled within her and returned the kiss in total abandon.

"Hamburgers," he said finally, his voice raspy.

"I suppose. Does the landlord know about Homer?"

"Yep. There's a grassy courtyard on the other side where Homer can exercise. Let's go. I'm starving."

"Okay." She turned to glance around the room once more. It really was lovely. She felt much calmer now and knew she had no reason to be upset.

But as she left the apartment with Joseph, she was frowning.

To Kendra's amazement, Joseph voiced no objection to her proposed plan that they take both cars to Port Payne in order to transport more of their belongings.

"You don't want to argue about my making the drive?" she said as they ate hamburgers and French fries.

"Nope."

"I'll be darned."

"Due to the fact that you won't be out of my sight on that empty stretch of road."

"Keep it up, Bennett," she said. "You'll be eligible for the chauvinist-of-the-year award."

At the cabins in Port Payne, Kendra entered her living room, while Joseph headed next door. She packed her car in an orderly fashion, taking what she would need to spend the night, a box of food from the kitchen and whatever else would fit.

"How are you coming?" Joseph called as he crossed the lawn.

"Not too badly. I shipped some of my things out here, so we'll have to make more than one trip."

"No problem. We'll just get the rest later. We'll come up on the weekend and say goodbye to everyone. I have

all my stuff in my car. Give me that box. I have room
for it. Say now, here's the famous baseball bat.''

"Oh, darn, I didn't leave room for my geraniums.''

"We'll get them next time. Let's hit the road. We still
have to unload all this junk, you know.''

Kendra locked the door of the cabin and stood in the
dark on the porch for a long moment. She'd come to
this cabin so filled with dreams. She had wanted to be
the finest teacher, the most independent, in-charge
young woman to swoop into Michigan in a decade. Instead, she was floundering in her role of teacher, stum-
bling in her steps toward independence.

But she was loved by the most magnificent man
imaginable. The future, their future together, was a
hazy blur, but somehow they would work everything
out. As equal partners, they would move forward.

A chill wind swept across the porch, and Kendra
shivered. A sense of foreboding crept in around her
again, and she hunched her shoulders beneath her coat.
Why did she feel this way? She was doing exactly what
she wanted to do. But she had a mental image of her
independence slipping through her fingers like quick-
silver. No, that wasn't fair. Joseph had done nothing
wrong!

"Kendra? Where are you?" he called from the car.

"What? Oh, I'm here, Joseph, just locking the
door.''

"Ready to go?" he asked, coming to the bottom of
the steps.

"All set.''

"Okay, same plan. I'll follow you back to Bay City.
I'll unload both cars once we get to the apartment.''

"Don't be silly. I'll carry my things in.''

"You've had a tough enough day as it is, Kendra. Think about a long soak in a bubble bath. Sound good?"

"Heavenly. And I'll do just that after I unload my car." She was firm.

"Nope, Homer and I are in charge of car-unloading. You can make up the bed. His voice became lower. "Our bed—the one I'm going to meet you in when you're soft and satiny and smell oh-so-lovely after that bubble bath."

"You don't play fair," she said, feeling the warm flush of her cheeks.

Joseph reached up, grabbed her around the waist and lifted her off of the porch.

"But you love me," he said, close to her lips.

"Yes. Oh, yes, Joseph, I do."

"Let's go home."

Seven

The next morning, as Kendra shut off the alarm, she opened one eye to glare at the offending clock. An instant later both eyes flew open as she realized she had no idea where she was.

Oh, yes, she thought foggily after a few seconds of panic, the apartment in Bay City.

Kendra yawned.

The apartment in Bay City, in bed with Joseph Bennett, her thoughts continued.

Kendra turned her head, and her nose nearly bumped into Joseph's. He was sleeping on his stomach, and a soft smile formed on Kendra's lips.

How she loved this man. Their lovemaking of the previous night had been exquisite. Joseph had come into the bathroom while she'd been relaxing in the bubble bath. Without speaking, he had taken the washcloth and gently stroked her back, her arms, her breasts, then...

"Heavens," Kendra said as new feelings of desire crept through her.

"Hmm?" Joseph mumbled.

"Shhh, you're sleeping."

"I am?" he asked, opening his eyes. "Then who are you talking to?"

"Me. I'm sorry I woke you. I've got to get ready for school. Go back to sleep," she whispered.

Joseph's hand slid across her bare stomach, then inched upward to fondle one breast.

"Some things are much nicer than sleep," he said, his voice husky.

"I don't have time to—Joseph!"

"But you don't have to drive into Bay City. You're already here," he said with inarguable logic.

"Oh, that's a thought. I forgot about that. Well, I think I'll snooze for another half hour or so."

His hand moved to her other breast.

"Okay," he said. "You snooze. I'll just keep on with what I'm doing here. It's homework for a course I'm taking in anatomy by braille."

Kendra laughed, and in the next instant Joseph covered her body with his, his mouth melting over hers.

When Kendra left the apartment to drive to school, there was a flush on her cheeks and a sparkle in her eyes.

Neither that day nor the next brought a miraculous cure to the temperaments of Kendra's students. There were no further enthusiastic debates on any topic, nor was any interest shown in history. They were simply two grimly routine days at school, and Kendra wore what was becoming her customary frown. Each night, as she drove to the apartment, she pushed aside her increasing depression regarding her teaching, only to have the frown return when she arrived.

On Thursday she was greeted by Joseph and the announcement that he had driven to Port Payne, gotten the key from Mr. Anderson and brought the remaining things from her cabin. The geraniums stood in a neat row on the counter, out of Homer's reach.

Friday she arrived home to discover the kitchen stocked with food and telephones installed in the living room and bedroom. Kendra insisted that they were overdue on discussing dividing up the expenses. Joseph breezily said they'd figure it out later. There was a science-fiction movie showing in town, he said, and if they hurried through dinner they could get there in time.

Kendra had difficulty concentrating on the film as she replayed in her mind the events of the past two days. Again, she realized, Joseph had done nothing wrong. He had simply been Joseph, moving full steam ahead, getting the job done. She had thanked him for bringing her belongings from Port Payne, yet her smile had been forced.

She was being too sensitive, Kendra told herself. Joseph's days were free and hers were not, and he'd simply done what needed doing. She was being childish and foolish to be annoyed that she'd had no choice in the color, location or number of telephones to be installed in the apartment. The food he had purchased was all to her liking. No, Joseph had done nothing wrong. But . . .

She was doing nothing more than chasing her own thoughts, Kendra decided. Going around and around in an endless circle, attempting to find fault with Joseph's actions, then realizing there was no blame to place. If only she could relax, quit questioning every-thing he did.

"You're awfully quiet tonight," Joseph said as they entered the apartment after the movie. "Is anything wrong?"

"No." She took off her coat and hung it up.

"That was a great movie," Joseph said. "The little kid stole the show. Man, I love kids. I wish you were pregnant with my baby right now."

"You're joking!" Kendra exclaimed, an incredulous expression on her face. "You'd be in Detroit, and I'd be here trying to explain to the school board why one of their unmarried teachers was turning into a water-melon."

"Don't be silly." He sat down next to her. "You'd be in Detroit with me, as my wife."

"What?" Her voice rose. "I have a contract for the entire school year."

"I'm an attorney, remember? I know how to nego-tiate the breaking of contracts. In fact, I wanted to talk to you about that. I'm sure Rick is going to lighten up on me as soon as he checks me over. I don't want to leave you here alone any longer than necessary when I go back to Detroit. I figure I can get a compromise for you from the school board and have you released from your contract before Christmas, when the semester ends. We could get married during the holidays and get serious about making that baby."

A rushing noise filled Kendra's ears, and she stared at Joseph as though he were a stranger who had sud-denly appeared in her living room.

"Kendra? You're awfully pale. Are you sure you're not catching something? Would you like to go crawl into bed?"

"I have no intention—" she was so angry her voice was trembling "—of breaking my contract. I don't recall your having asked me to marry you. And did it occur to you that I might not be ready to have a baby?"

"Hey, calm down," he said, patting her hand. "We don't need to cover all this tonight, when you're coming down with something."

"I'm not coming down with anything!" she yelled, jumping to her feet. "You've gone too far this time, Joseph. I'm not a geranium you can pick up and move at will."

"What in the hell is that supposed to mean?" he demanded none too quietly.

"I hate that brown phone!" Kendra shouted, pointing at the offending instrument. And then in the next breath, with volume set on high, she burst into tears.

"Oh, man," Joseph groaned, then lunged to his feet and put his arms around Kendra. He eased her close to his chest, then nestled her head against his shoulder. She cried with loud, gulping sobs as she buried her face in his sweater.

"There, there, don't cry," Joseph said in a soothing voice. "I'm going to tuck you in bed and get you an aspirin. I'm going to take very good care of you, and you'll feel better in the morning."

"I'm losing it," she said, tears streaming down her face as she pulled out of his grasp.

"You're not losing it. You're all worn out. I'm going to put you to bed and—"

"No! No, no. It's control of my life—that's what I'm losing. You're taking it away from me, Joseph, piece by piece. I decide to do something and you've already done it—just the way I was going to do it, so I can't complain, because I'd sound like a dimwit. How would you feel if I brought your underwear and geraniums from Port Payne?''

"I beg your pardon," he said, frowning.

"How am I going to learn how to take care of myself if I don't get snowed in because I was too dumb to think about it?" she rushed on. "I don't hate that phone. It looks like a huge piece of chocolate fudge. But I didn't get to pick it!" And the tears started again.

"Kendra, honey, don't cry." He took a step toward her.

"No," she said, backing up. "You've got to listen to me."

"I'm trying to." He raked a hand through his hair. "But you're not making any sense."

"Joseph," she said, brushing the tears from her cheeks with shaking hands, "it's happening, don't you see? Little by little you're taking over my life. You're doing everything for me. Everything. Now you've gone too far. You're talking about our entire future as though it's all settled. You have me breaking my contract, marrying you, moving to Detroit and getting pregnant."

"I love you," he said, his jaw tightening. "I've been wracking my brain to come up with a way we can be together. And that's wrong?"

"Yes. No. I don't know." Kendra threw up her hands and sniffled. "I just want to have a voice, be part of the decision-making, not hear about it all after the fact. My job is important to me and—"

"I know that," he interrupted her. "And I also know that it's ripping you up because it's not going the way you dreamed. Kendra, would you actually hate leaving a place that depresses you, makes you feel like a failure five days a week? Your education, your mind, wouldn't be wasted. You could do something else instead of being emotionally abused by teenagers.''

"But—''

"We'll be together as husband and wife. I want you with me, Kendra.''

"What about what I want?'' she yelled.

Joseph stiffened, and he suddenly appeared pale beneath his tan. Anger flashed through his dark eyes. He took a deep breath and let it out slowly. Then his shoulders seemed to slump as a flicker of pain crossed his features.

"I thought—'' his voice was oddly husky "—that you wanted to be with me, too. That you wanted to be my wife, have my babies. I thought that was what love is all about—two people being together.''

"Yes, of course, it is, but...I don't know how to make you understand. I really don't. I try to explain it and I end up sounding so foolish. I'm confused and upset and I need some room, some time to sort this all through. I love you, Joseph, but...''

"But what?'' he said, tensing again as he frowned.

"I... Oh, boy,'' she gasped as the telephone rang. "That phone can't be ringing. No one has this number.''

"My brothers do,'' Joseph said gruffly, and snatched up the receiver. "Yeah. Hello.... What?... When?... Matt, how bad is it?''

"Joseph?'' Kendra whispered, her eyes wide. "What's wrong?''

"What hospital?... Damn, he's got to be all right... Look, I'm on my way.... No, I won't sit here and wait for you to call.... I don't care what Rick said. I'm coming. It'll take me about three hours to drive down.... Yeah, yeah, I'll be careful on the roads. Matt, if you have any connections in high places like Mom thinks, use them!''

Joseph slammed the receiver into place, then ran his hand through his hair. "Dear God," he said in a hoarse voice.

"Joseph? What happened?"

"It's David," he told her, striding toward the bedroom. "He's been in a car accident. I've got to get to Detroit."

"Joseph," Kendra said, hurrying after him, "I heard what you said. Matt and Rick want you to wait here. Rick must be concerned about you making that drive under such stress. I'll drive you."

Joseph pulled a suitcase from the closet and began to throw things into it. Kendra watched, wringing her hands.

"Joseph, are you listening to me? Please let me drive you to Detroit."

"No," he said, continuing to pack. "There's no way to know what kind of weather I'll run into. I'd rather drive myself. Besides, this will give you the room, time, space—whatever it is you need to figure out what you want. Take care of Homer for me, will you?" he said, snapping the suitcase closed.

"Why are you doing this alone when it isn't necessary? You're putting yourself in danger."

"Because I love my brother," he said, his voice low. "Because I want to be with him, and no sacrifice is too great in order to accomplish that."

"Oh, Joseph," she said, fresh tears brimming her eyes.

He left the room, snatching up his jacket as he went.

Kendra was right behind him. "Joseph," she said, "will you call me when you get there so I'll know you arrived all right? And to tell me how your brother is?"

"Yeah," he said, stopping at the door and turning to her.

"Please—please—drive carefully."

"I will. I've got to go," he said, his hand on the doorknob. "Ah, hell," he said, dropping his suitcase and jacket on the floor. He reached for Kendra and pulled her roughly into his arms, his mouth coming down on hers in a bruising kiss. "I love you," he said, his voice raspy. "Damn you, Kendra, don't forget how much I love you. Sort through whatever is confusing you, but remember how very much I love you."

And then he was gone.

For a long moment, Kendra stared at the closed door. She saw Joseph's face with crystal clarity, saw the pain in his eyes, pain that she knew was a combination of his heart-wrenching concern for his brother and his hurt and confusion over the jumbled accusations she'd hurled at him.

"What have I done?" she whispered, pressing her fingertips to her lips.

The tinkling of a bell brought her from her anguished thoughts, and she glanced down to see Homer sitting on her foot. She scooped up the rabbit and buried her face in his soft fur.

"Oh, Homer," she said, nearly choking on a sob, "I love him. I do! Oh, I'm so frightened."

Homer wiggled in her arms, and she set him back on the floor. He hopped to the door.

"All right," she said wearily, "I'll take you to the courtyard. Then I'm not budging from that phone, that beautiful chocolate-brown phone."

Kendra was chilled when she returned to the apartment with Homer. She glanced at the telephone, then ran a tubful of warm water. After her bath she donned a flannel nightie and her robe, then curled up in the corner of the sofa.

She felt like a stranger existing in her own body, a confused woman suddenly unsure of who she was, what she wanted. The only thing she was certain of was that she loved Joseph Bennett. "Poor man," she said dryly. "He's in love with a loony-tune."

Kendra sighed and stared at the telephone. She couldn't think any more tonight, she decided. She had to put everything from her mind and wait for Joseph to call. He shouldn't have made that long drive under the stress of worrying about David, she thought anxiously, and after the scene she had caused. Rick had wanted Joseph to stay in Bay City, but not stubborn Joseph. He was off and running, full steam ahead because . . .

Because I love my brother. Because I want to be with him, and no sacrifice is too great in order to accomplish that.

No sacrifice is too great. . . .

No sacrifice is too great. . . .

"Stop it," she said, pressing her fingertips to her throbbing temples.

She drew a steadying breath, then got to her feet, determined to escape the taunting voices in her mind. She'd have a cup of tea, take two aspirins and wait for Joseph to call.

With agonizing slowness the seconds became minutes, then hours. Kendra paced, slouched on the sofa, then paced again, back and forth, staring at the telephone and willing it to ring. It had been nearly four hours since Joseph had left the apartment when the shrill sound shattered the heavy silence. Kendra snatched up the receiver.

"Hello?" she said breathlessly.

"It's Joseph."

"Oh, thank God," she said, sinking onto the sofa. "Are you all right?"

"Yes."

"And David? How is he, Joseph?"

"He... Kendra, he's—" Joseph said his voice breaking "—in a coma. He's connected to machines, has tubes.... The doctors don't know if he's going...to make it."

"Oh, Joseph, I'm so sorry. Is everyone there?"

"Everyone but you. No, forget that. That wasn't fair. Ah, damn, I feel as though they're looking at me to fix this, make it all right, take charge like I've always done, but I'm helpless, Kendra. I want to slam someone up against the wall and demand he save my brother's life. I love David—we all love David—but it isn't making any difference! Isn't love supposed to make a difference?"

"Joseph, I..." Kendra started as tears spilled onto her cheeks. She wanted to go to him, comfort him, but he'd told her to use their time apart to sort through her confusion. If she went to Detroit now, he might view her as yet another problem he had to deal with. She'd leave him alone so he could concentrate on David.

"Ah, hell," Joseph said, sounding totally exhausted, "I'm dumping on you because I'm trying to be strong for everyone else. Look, I'm just babbling, not making any sense. I'll call you later. I love you. Goodbye, Kendra."

"Joseph, I..." The dial tone buzzed in Kendra's ear. "...love you, too." She slowly replaced the receiver.

And then she cried.

Kendra cried for Joseph, who was suffering such anguish over his brother. She cried for David, even though she had never met him. And she cried for herself, because she was alone and frightened and losing touch once again with who she was. She cried until she was numb, then stumbled into the bedroom, flung herself across the bed and slept.

At eleven o'clock the next morning, Joseph called again. There was no change in David's condition, he said, and the doctors were still reluctant to make a prognosis.

"Have you slept?" Kendra asked.

"Not yet. Rick is hauling me out of here now. We talked our folks into going home for a while. David's wife won't budge."

"I can understand that," Kendra said softly.

"I've got to go, Kendra. I'll call you later."

"Take care of yourself, Joseph, please. I love you."

"Yeah, I love you, too. Bye."

Kendra sighed as she replaced the receiver, then kept her hand on the smooth plastic, not wishing to break the only link she had to Joseph. He had sounded so tired, she thought, so defeated. She wanted to hold him in her arms, comfort him, be there with him. At least Rick was insisting that Joseph rest. If Joseph got stubborn about it, Matt would probably outmuscle him into complying. Oh, how intensely they loved, those Bennetts. And one of them loved her.

By two o'clock, Kendra was so restless and edgy that her teeth ached from clenching them. She'd left the apartment only long enough to take Homer to the courtyard, then hurried back to sit by the telephone. She was operating on the theory that no news was good news and told herself that Joseph was getting his much-needed sleep.

On impulse she dialed information, asking for the number of Libby's store in Port Payne. Kendra had no idea if Libby had even gone to Port Payne for the weekend, and she didn't want to tie up the telephone line for long, but she needed desperately to talk to someone. When Libby answered on the third ring, a nearly hysterical giggle escaped from Kendra's throat.

"It's Kendra," she said. "I . . . Libby, I . . ."

"Hey, what's wrong?" Libby asked. "Everyone here is in a flutter of excitement because you and Joseph moved to Bay City together. I'm so happy for you, sweetie. But you sound frantic."

"Joseph's brother was in an accident, Joseph went to Detroit, and I had just pitched a fit because I'm not a geranium," Kendra said, pressing her hand to her forehead. "I'm so confused about who I am and what I want. Joseph is exhausted, and I'm worried about him. And there's nothing I can do to help except take care of Homer."

"Who? Never mind. Put the coffeepot on, cookie. I'm coming to visit. What's your address?"

"Oh, Libby, thank you," Kendra said, going limp against the sofa cushions. "Thank you."

When Libby arrived, Kendra greeted her with a hug, then introduced her to Homer.

"Well, hello, Homer," Libby said, a disbelieving expression on her face.

"He thinks he's a cat," Kendra explained.

"He's an extremely handsome rabbit. Unusual pet for around the house, but then I get the feeling that

Joseph Bennett is not an ordinary man. Am I safe in assuming that you're in love with him?''

"Homer?''

"Joseph! Lord, Kendra, you're coming unglued. Sit down and tell all.''

"I'll get your coffee,'' Kendra offered.

"No,'' Libby said, nearly pushing Kendra onto the sofa, ''I'll do it. Homer, you devil, I saw you wink at me. Been training with a master, have you?''

Libby went into the kitchen and returned with the tray Kendra had set out on the counter. Libby placed the offering of coffee and cookies on the end table, then sat on the opposite end of the sofa from Kendra.

"Okay,'' Libby said gently. ''What has you in such a dither?''

And Kendra told her. While pacing back and forth across the room and wringing her hands, she related Joseph's actions, her reactions and Joseph's full-steam-ahead plans for their future. She spoke of her frustrations over her inability to reach her students and of her lack of foresight in questioning Mr. Anderson about the availability of a snowplow in Port Payne. She admitted her confusion and her fears, fears of losing herself, of being swept up once again into a protective cocoon, and of being unable to speak in a voice that would be heard.

"I see,'' Libby said when Kendra finally stopped speaking.

"Do I sound like I should be shipped to the farm?'' Kendra asked miserably.

"No,'' Libby said, laughing softly, ''you sound like a woman who is in love with and loved by a very dynamic, take-charge-type guy. Joseph knows what he wants, moves in and gets the job done.''

"That's no joke," Kendra said dryly. "Covering all details, too. Like fudge-colored telephones. Oh, what's wrong with me? I love Joseph, but I have such fears and doubts, and I can't make him understand. That's because I sound like an idiot whenever I try to explain what I'm feeling."

"I understand perfectly, but then I'm a woman. I'm not saying men are dense... Well, some are...but they do operate on a different wavelength at times. By the same token, I think you're overdoing your stand on independence."

"What?" Kendra said, sitting bolt upright. "That's not a very nice thing to say."

"Kendra, when my husband died, I was left with an enormous house, a seat on the board of directors of his company, a stockbroker, staff of lawyers—the works. I felt I owed it to George to step into his shoes and take his place. After about six months I was miserable. I looked in the mirror one morning and asked myself who in hell's bells I was. I was walking, Kendra, in shoes that didn't fit. I sold everything and got out."

"And?"

"I bought a lovely condo in Midland, my place in Port Payne, and started my stained-glass business. I did what I wanted to do, was true to myself."

"That's what I'm trying to do, Libby," she insisted.

"Are you?" Libby said.

"Yes. Teaching was my dream. I worked hard for that degree and for my independence."

"Why?"

"Why?" Kendra frowned, thinking, "Well, because... because I wasn't happy in the world I was existing in."

"So you created another world in your mind, the perfect place. You would teach, function on your own, be everything you hadn't been before. Oh, Kendra, hasn't it occurred to you that those might be the wrong shoes for you?"

"But—"

"Aren't you still trying to prove things to your parents? To admit that you made a career mistake probably seems to you like saying they'd been right all along. It takes more courage and independence to change boats in the middle of the stream than to complete the entire rocky ride."

"I think I'm going to cry again." Kendra sniffled.

"Tears are marvelous, as long as you know when to stop. Kendra, I can see that Joseph needs to slow down a bit, listen to you, be willing to compromise. But from where I'm sitting, you're the one who's refusing to budge. You're holding on to a tarnished dream of being a teacher because you're too frightened to let go. You're not accepting the love of a man who wants to cherish and—"

"Protect me."

"Damn right. My doctor friend in Midland insists I call him when I arrive in Port Payne so he knows I got there safely. Protective? Yes. And, oh, what a lovely, warm feeling I get knowing he cares. And I'm there for him when he's had a hard day. I add a feminine touch to his life, and our relationship is working out perfectly."

"That's beautiful," Kendra admitted.

"Think about it, Kendra. Oh, sweetie, don't you see? It's truth time, Kendra Smith. Your future happiness depends on your being honest with yourself.

"Oh, dear," Kendra said, pressing her hands to her cheeks.

"You're going to be all right, Kendra, so long as you're completely honest with yourself."

"Thank you so much, Libby," Kendra said, hugging her. "You're a wonderful friend."

"And Joseph could be your best friend, as well as your lover, if you let him. Choose your shoes wisely."

"Yes. Yes, I will."

Later, when Kendra closed the door behind her, Libby's words seemed to tumble together in her mind.

"No," she said, opening her eyes, "I've had enough of this confusion." She would, she told herself firmly, discover who Kendra Smith really was. She would find the shoes she was meant to wear and in the process find herself.

Homer hopped to the door.

"You want to go out again? Homer, is there something going on in that courtyard that I don't know about?" she said, her mood lightening.

Outside, Kendra filled her lungs with cold air, then smiled in delight when snowflakes began to drift down from the gray sky.

It was all so different from California, she mused. A total change in environment. What hadn't really changed was herself. She was still attempting to please others, to do what was expected of her. Yes, her role was different, but her attitude wasn't. She had, indeed, chosen new shoes, and they obviously didn't fit. It was time to start over again.

As six o'clock that evening, Joseph called.

"Kendra, David came out of the coma," he said, not bothering to say hello. "He's awake. The doctors are being very cautious in their prognosis, but it looks like he's going to be all right."

"Oh, Joseph, that's wonderful. Thank God. Did they allow you to see him?"

"Just for a few minutes. He has a number of broken bones, and bruises from head to toe, as well as a nasty concussion. He's crabby as hell, which means he's acting like himself. His wife told him to pipe down or she'd break more bones. There are smiling Bennetts in this town tonight; I can tell you that. I miss you. I want to hold you in my arms, kiss you, make love to you."

"Oh," Kendra said, swallowing heavily as desire tingled within her.

Joseph chuckled. "There you go with that articulate reply again."

"Well, I miss you, too. If you were here, Joseph, I'd kiss you until you couldn't breathe. I'd kiss every inch of you. Then my hands would—"

"Enough," he ordered her. "I'm dying. It was easier on my libido when you only said 'Oh.'"

"Don't you want to know what I was going to do with my hands?"

"No! I'm changing the subject for the sake of my sanity. Kendra, David is concerned about the case he took over for me when I went to Port Payne. We've got a nervous witness that David is afraid will bolt if we ask for a postponement. I assured David that I'd step back in and keep this thing on schedule."

"But you're not supposed to be working yet, Joseph."

"Once we knew David was going to be all right, Rick and his muscle man Matt hauled me over to Rick's office. I checked out with flying colors. I'm A-okay. Rick says it's due to his brilliance. He's such a pain."

"You're really all right?"

"Yep. Rick read me the riot act about working too hard in the future, and that was that. Case closed. Thing is, Kendra, I've got to stay here and prepare to go to trial on this case late next week. Our client deserves the best I can offer."

"Yes, of course he does."

"But, Kendra, you deserve the best I can offer, too, because I love you. So far I seem to have a lousy track record with you. I want to come back to Bay City right now and figure all this out with you, but I can't."

"I understand. I really do," she said sincerely.

"Well, you said you needed space and . . . Damn it, I don't like this. I won't be there, in that space, to tell you, show you, how much I love you. Kendra, I'm scared to death that you'll think it all through and decide you don't want me in your life," he admitted.

"I love you, Joseph."

"Yeah, well, I love you, too. I just hope that's enough. I'm depressing myself here. I'll call you tomorrow. Is Homer treating you okay?"

"He's super."

"Good. Think about me, Kendra. Good night."

"Good night, Joseph," she said softly, then replaced the receiver. Oh, yes, she'd think about Joseph Bennett, and she'd miss Joseph Bennett. But the majority of her mental energies, she knew, would be spent discovering which shoes she was meant to wear.

Eight

When Kendra took Homer outside on Sunday morning, she gasped at what she saw. Bay City had been transformed into a fairyland of snow stretching as far as the eye could see. Kendra romped with Homer in the courtyard until she was convinced her toes were frozen.

Deciding she was acting silly, but not caring, she placed a snowball in the freezer of the refrigerator. It was the first snowball she'd made in her entire twenty-six years, and it deserved to be preserved.

"So there," she said, patting the freezer door. The telephone rang, and she rushed to answer it. "Hello."

"Hi, Joseph Bennett here. Can't talk. I'm in a rush. I have to go to the law library."

"How nice," Kendra said, smiling.

"No, how boring. It's the only part of this career I hate. What I do at the law library, you see, is dig into dusty old books to find cases similar to the one I'm working on. That is what is known as history. Are you familiar with history? Of course you are. You love the stuff.'' He rambled on, not letting her get a word in edgewise. "Oh, how much simpler my life would be if I had someone to do this history junk for me. Well, it was nice talking to you. I love you. Bye.''

"Joseph?" Kendra said to the dial tone. "Joseph?" Law library? She repeated to herself. History of old cases? Joseph needed someone to uncover the information he had to have for his cases? Had he been saying that that someone could be her? she wondered, her mind racing.

Slow down, she told herself. Just slow down. She had one hundred and sixteen report cards to fill out, and everything else had to go on hold. History of old cases? Good Lord, how exciting and—

"Report cards, Kendra," she told herself sternly. "Now."

For the entire afternoon, except for taking Homer outside, Kendra did nothing but the paperwork that was due in the principal's office the next morning. As the hours passed, her depression deepened. A large number of students had failed the first quarter. If they didn't buckle down for the second one, they might not pass the course, and they wouldn't graduate.

"Why don't they care?" Kendra asked out loud. "Why can't I make them care?"

The telephone rang, and Kendra told herself she wouldn't let Joseph become aware of her gloomy mood. Her greeting was bright and cheerful, but it wasn't Joseph calling.

"Kendra?" a male voice said.

"Yes."

"This is Rick Bennett.''

"Oh, no. What's wrong with Joseph," she demanded, her heart pounding. "He told me you said he was all right now."

"He is, due to the fact that I allowed him the honor of being my patient. Yeah, he's fine. Ugly as ever, but fine. He's standing right here."

"But *you're* calling me," Kendra said, shaking her head slightly.

"Yeah, because Joseph has laryngitis, can't say a word. It's caused by the dust he inhaled at the law library today. Do you know about law libraries?"

Kendra smiled.

"Strange places, those law libraries," Rick went on. "They're jam-packed with history...and dust, of course. Well, I'm supposed to tell you that Joseph loves you. So, Kendra, Joseph loves you. Got that? Poor devil, his throat is killing him. I tell him to stay out of that law library with all that history and all that dust. But does he listen? Hell, no. Gotta go. We have to beat up on David because he's threatening to tear the hospital apart if they don't let him out. Matt will handle him. Joseph and I will just stand there and growl."

"Rick, thank you," she said. "Tell Joseph I love him, too."

"Aw, isn't that sweet? I don't have to kiss him for you, do I? Boy, he makes my life miserable. If only he'd stay away from that history and dust. See ya, Kendra. Bye."

"Goodbye," she said, laughing. Joseph meant it, her heart sang. He really meant that there could be a place for her working by his side in a field she adored. Oh, dear heaven, how she loved him.

At seven o'clock Monday night, Kendra heard from another Bennett.

"Hello," she answered the phone.

"Kendra? Matt Bennett."

"Hello, Matt," she said, smiling. "Oh, I guess I should call you Father."

"Naw, no need. Every time someone calls me Father, I look over my shoulder to see if my dad just walked into the room. Okay, down to business. Joseph said to tell you he loves you. He's getting his voice back, but he's afraid to use it over the phone for fear he'll be arrested as a heavy breather."

Kendra burst into laughter.

"Next up," Matt said. "I have a problem. Bet you didn't think that priests had problems, huh? Believe me, just being a Bennett is a problem. Anyway, I'm working on my sermon for Sunday that I'm giving as the guest priest at a home for delinquent boys. I want to make the point that claiming they got into drugs, quit school—whatever—because of today's social pressures is a cop-out. I need to show that each era in history had its pressures. Get it?"

"Yes. Yes, I do," Kendra said, her blue eyes sparkling with excitement.

"History is not my strong suit. History is boring."

"And dusty," Kendra added.

"That, too. Can you bail me out, Kendra? What grim stuff happened way back when that I can use as examples?"

"Do you have a pencil?"

"I'm ready, kid. Lay it on me."

For the next half hour, Kendra told story after story to Matt about social struggles in earlier times.

"Fantastic," Matt said finally. "You are a life-saver."

"I'm glad I could help."

On Tuesday morning, a teacher's aide delivered a sealed envelope to Kendra in her classroom. The note enclosed stated that Jane Fletcher, the principal, wished to speak with Kendra in the office after the last class of the day. Before long, Kendra developed a tension headache and a knot in her stomach. It was a hideously long day.

Jane Fletcher, a stout woman in her sixties, had a soft voice and a ready smile. The smile was nowhere in evidence when Kendra sat down in the chair opposite the principal's desk.

"Kendra," Jane said, "I'll get right to the point. I was deeply troubled by the number of students failing your class this grading period."

"As was I," Kendra said, hoping, praying, her voice was steady.

"I did a comparison of the grades your students are receiving in their other classes. Some are failing across the board and have obviously put their graduation in jeopardy. But many that you failed are receiving a C or better in all other subjects. And so I have to look further to find out what the problem is."

"I understand."

"Kendra, what happened? When you interviewed for this position, you were like a bright candle burning with excitement to begin your new adventure. What can I do to help you?"

"I simply need time to adjust to teaching students who..." Kendra stopped speaking and drew a deep breath. "No, that's not true," she said, looking directly at Mrs. Fletcher. "My love of history hasn't diminished, but I think I lack the ability to relate it to those kids in a way that creates any kind of enthusiasm. They're bored, and I don't blame them. I have chosen—" Kendra's voice trembled slightly "—the wrong career. It's time I faced that fact."

Mrs. Fletcher studied Kendra for a long moment. Kendra's heartbeat echoed in her ears as she kept her hands clutched tightly in her lap.

"My dear," the principal said finally, "as sorry as I am to say this, you're right. You don't belong here, Kendra."

"But I have a contract, a commitment to you and the school board. I'd feel as though I were shirking my responsibility if I didn't teach all the way till June."

"We have many qualified teachers who are substituting because there simply weren't enough jobs to go around. I should have no difficulty finding a replacement for you within a few days. I do hope you'll be happy in your next endeavor, Kendra."

"Thank you, Mrs. Fletcher," she said, getting to her feet. "Thank you more than I can say."

"Goodbye, dear. I'll let you know the moment your replacement is hired."

"Goodbye," Kendra said, hurrying from the room as tears filled her eyes.

Free! Free! Free!

The words tingled like wind chimes in Kendra's mind as she gathered her belongings and dashed out of the school to her car. The nightmare was over. She had admitted that she had made a mistake. Lightning hadn't struck her dead. The earth hadn't stopped spinning. She was alive and free. She wasn't a quitter; she was a woman who had listened to the voice of her heart and faced the truth of her error.

Oh, how she wanted to share it all with Joseph and tell him that she would never again wear the ill-fitting shoes of the teacher. She was a barefoot wonder at the moment, wearing no shoes at all, but for now, it felt wonderful.

In her apartment, Kendra scooped up Homer, gave him a loud, smacking kiss on the nose and decided he had smiled. She took him for a romp in the snow.

When Joseph called at nine o'clock, he sounded tired, and Kendra immediately expressed her concern.

"I'm fine," he said. "Even have a voice. I won't deny this is a hectic week, getting ready for the trial. I have to report in to David at the hospital every two seconds, or he fusses and fumes. The case is solid, though. It should go well. Damn, the other phone is ringing. I'd better get it."

"Are you still at the office?"

"Yeah. Love ya. Bye."

"Joseph, I . . . Goodbye," she said, frowning. She hadn't had a chance to tell him her news. Well, she'd rather tell him in person, anyway. But when would she have that opportunity? Every spare minute Joseph had was spent preparing for the trial. How exciting it would be to watch him in action in the courtroom. He'd be magnificent, she was sure. The jury would be spell-bound. "Wait a minute," she said. "Why can't I see him in the courtroom? Homer, the minute my replacement is hired, you and I are going for a ride."

When Joseph called on Wednesday night, he seemed preoccupied. After Kendra had commented three times on the weather before getting a vague "Yeah, it snowed" from Joseph, she decided it was not the time to announce her momentous news about leaving teaching. She still preferred to tell him in person, and she would when she arrived in Detroit.

"Joseph, are you all right?" she asked finally.

"What? Oh, sure, I'm fine. I'm waiting for a call from the opposing attorney."

"Oh?"

"My client is accused of trying to murder his wife for her insurance. This is confidential, okay? We have a witness that will give the old boy an airtight alibi."

"Really? This is better than the movies."

Joseph chuckled. "I wouldn't go that far. It's a simple case of a jealous wife who's had enough of her husband's playing around."

"So she accuses him of attempted murder?" Kendra asked, astounded.

"Yep."

"But he's innocent?"

"He was with his mistress. She's a topless dancer. Did I mention that my client is seventy-eight years old?"

"Oh, good grief," Kendra said.

"Anyway, David and I agreed to give the opposition one last chance to drop the charges. They're conferring right now. I'm at my apartment, so I'd better free up this line."

"Oh, yes, of course."

"Kendra, I miss you like hell."

"I miss you, too."

"I'd better go. I love you."

"And I love you. Good night, Joseph," she said, then replaced the receiver. Drop the charges? she mused. Then there wouldn't be a trial. Well, no matter. She'd drive into Detroit anyway, just as soon as she could.

After school on Thursday, Mrs. Fletcher came to Kendra's classroom with a young, good-looking man and introduced him as the teacher who was taking her place. With a surge of relief, Kendra handed over her grade books and left the school, a smile on her face.

She was up at dawn the next morning. She dressed in her suede suit, then packed a small suitcase. Homer had his fling in the courtyard, then Kendra ate a light breakfast as she studied a map of how to get to Detroit. She set her suitcase by the door, then decided to water the geraniums before she left.

She'd just replaced the watering can in the kitchen and returned to the living room, when she gasped and stopped in her tracks. Her eyes widened as she heard a key being inserted in the door, then Joseph entered the apartment.

"Joseph," she said. "You scared me to death. What are you doing here?"

"I live here, remember? The charges were dropped against my client, so..." His gaze fell on her suitcase, and his jaw clenched. "Going somewhere?" he said, frowning deeply.

"Well, yes, I was planning on—"

"On what?" he said, shrugging out of his jacket and tossing it onto a chair. "Taking off to parts unknown to find your almighty space?"

"How can you say such a thing?" she asked angrily.

"Oh, I get it," he said, a sarcastic edge to his voice. "You're such a dedicated teacher you've decided to spend the night at the school to soak up educational vibes. Why the swanky suit, Kendra? Did you hope to dazzle your students into learning something?''

"Joseph, don't," she said quietly. "You're obviously tired, and you're saying things you don't mean. Why don't you sleep for a while, then—"

"Don't patronize me. I want to know what in the hell is going on here."

"I was coming to Detroit!" she yelled, matching his volume, "to watch you in the courtroom."

"I told you the other night that the charges might be dropped."

"Either way, we would have been together."

"What about your job?" he roared.

"I quit!"

Kendra cringed as she watched every muscle in Joseph's body tense. She had the irrational thought that his jaw must ache from how tightly he was clenching it.

"You did what?" he asked in carefully measured words.

"I quit."

"You quit," he repeated, nodding. "Let me make sure I have this straight," he said, raising his hand to silence her. "You stood in this room throwing a holy fit when I suggested I negotiate to get you out of your contract at the end of the semester. Then, on your own, because we all know how independent you are, you up and quit? Told them to stuff it, and left?"

"No! Not exactly. I had a wonderful talk with Mrs. Fletcher, the principal, and we agreed that I didn't belong there. I wasn't meant to be a teacher, Joseph. I admit that now."

"But when I said all that you freaked out, accused me of trying to control your life. I was afraid to open my mouth around you for fear I'd set you off again. I can't believe this," he said, raking a hand through his hair. "I leave town, and you quit."

"Yes, I did. It was time I faced the truth about having made the wrong career choice."

"What other great revelations did you have while I was gone?" he demanded, glaring at her.

"Isn't that enough? Joseph, this was a major change in my life."

"No joke. Would you care to share your future plans with me?"

"Well, I don't really have any yet. I thought that maybe... Well, you were certainly clear enough about the possibility of my working with you doing research for your cases."

"Oh, that plan met with your approval, huh?" he said dryly. "Well, score one for Bennett."

"Joseph, I don't understand why you're acting this way. Maybe I missed something, but I thought you'd be pleased that I'd finally admitted I didn't belong in teaching. I've made a major decision in my life."

"That's it in a nutshell, kid. You made the decision. I was rotten to the core every time I suggested it, but it's hunky-dory when it's your idea. What's next? *You've* decided we should get married? Oh, and when are we having our first baby? Be sure to let me know."

Tears sprung to Kendra's eyes, and she blinked them away, refusing to give in to the icy misery sweeping through her. Everything was falling apart, going wrong, and she didn't understand why. This was a nightmare!

"I've had enough of this," Joseph said, starting across the room. "I've got to get some sleep. I was counting the hours until I could be here with you and... Hell," he said, slamming the bedroom door closed.

"Well, hell to you, too," Kendra said, planting her hands on her hips. Oh-h-h, she fumed, what an infuriating man. She'd quit her teaching job, which was exactly what he'd wanted, and he was all bent out of shape. "Wait a minute," she said, suddenly realizing what had happened.

She had hurt Joseph's masculine pride.

When Joseph had been one step ahead of her in knowing what needed doing, Kendra realized, *her* pride had been wounded. She'd felt controlled, robbed of her voice in decisions. She'd ranted in anger, but no sooner had he left Bay City than she'd turned right around and done what he'd been suggesting in the first place!

How clear it all was now, Kendra thought, staring at the closed bedroom door. She'd flung Joseph's offer to help her break her contract back in his face. She'd brutally rejected his hopes and dreams of their marrying and having a baby. Yet at that very moment her thoughts were centered on being Joseph's wife and having his child. Her timing, her acceptance of his actions, had once again been off kilter. She'd moved slower than full-steam-ahead Bennett, and now she was paying the price.

But how, Kendra wondered, was she to make Joseph understand that they were at last working toward the same goal? The pieces of their lives could now fit together like a jigsaw puzzle created by a master craftsman. She could be his wife, the mother of his child, and still embrace her love of history by doing Joseph's research.

She had found her shoes, and they would fit perfectly.

"I am all grown up and doing fine," Kendra said softly. "At last."

Kendra got to her feet and walked to the closed bed-room door. I love you, Joseph, she thought. Then she turned and went into the kitchen. She had to keep busy, she decided, or she'd drive herself crazy. When Joseph woke up, they'd talk, get everything straightened out. They had to!

The aroma of chocolate-chip cookies baking in the oven drifted through the air a short time later. Kendra was thinking of the evening she'd taken the same kind of cookies to Joseph's cabin. So many changes had taken place since she'd first seen Homer eating the last geranium in the greenhouse.

In the days that had followed her first meeting with Joseph, Kendra had shared the most exquisite love-making she had ever known, with the only man she had ever loved. Joseph had awakened her femininity and had shown her the joys of womanhood.

Now, Kendra told herself, she had grown in mind as well. She was ready to be woman to Joseph's man in every sense of the word. She knew she could be his equal partner, half of a team.

Kendra gave Homer a cookie, then began to clean the kitchen. She had just finished wiping up the counters when Joseph appeared in the doorway. He was dressed only in his jeans, his dark hair in tousled disarray.

"Cookies," he said. "Smells good."

"Help yourself," Kendra told him. He was beauti-ful, she marveled. She wanted him to take her in his arms and ... "Would you like a glass of milk?" If only he'd kiss her, hold her. He hadn't even touched her since he'd been back. "Did you get enough sleep?"

"Yeah, I'm fine. I'll get the milk. Hey, Homer, how's life? World treating you okay, buddy?"

Kendra set a plate of cookies on the table in the eating area, then moved away as Joseph sat down with his glass of milk. A charged silence fell over the apartment. After ten minutes, Kendra had had enough.

"Joseph," she said, sitting opposite him at the table, "I think we should talk. Don't you?"

"You want my opinion?" he asked sarcastically, not looking at her. "Wonders never cease."

Kendra took a deep breath and told herself firmly that she must not punch him in the nose.

"Joseph," she began again, "I don't want to oversimplify our problems, but what we have here is a misunderstanding due to a basic lack of communication. Oh, and lousy timing."

"Do tell," he said, popping another cookie into his mouth.

"You told me once that it shouldn't matter who made decisions as long as we were both pleased with the outcome. Do you still believe that?"

"I suppose."

"So? I quit my job. I'm free to come to Detroit with you. I want to marry you and have your baby. Our dreams match up, Joseph. Isn't that what's important?"

"Yeah," he said, looking directly at her for the first time. "Except for the fact that I have a knot in my gut from wondering what we'll cross swords on next. I can't live my life weighing my words before I speak to you, worrying about whether I'll insult your independence or come across as too protective."

"It wouldn't be like that."

"How do I know? Tell me, Kendra, just how in the hell do I know that? If I brought you a sweater on a chilly evening, would you hug me or hit me? No, you'd probably ignore me, then go get your own sweater. I'd never know where I stood with you. I love you, Kendra, but I'm not sure I can live with you."

"Then maybe," she said, hearing the trembling in her voice, "you should test it out."

"Meaning?"

"We'll live together in Detroit. I'll work with you, do your research. We'll conduct our lives as though we were married, but we won't be married."

"My mother would put a contract out on my life," Joseph said, suddenly smiling. "Maybe Matt can get her a discount on candles if she buys them by the gross."

"Oh," Kendra said, frowning, "I wouldn't want to do anything to upset your family."

"I'm a big boy. They'll just have to accept that. Ah, Kendra," he said, sighing, "I don't know what went wrong here."

Pride, Kendra thought. Pride, timing and the wrong pair of shoes.

"All I know," Joseph went on, "is that I love you. Beyond that it's foggy, uncertain. I feel like I've fought a war, and I don't know why. Yeah, maybe you're right. We should slow down, really look at who we are as a couple. Okay, we'll do it. The landlord is going to think I'm nuts, but I'll tell him we're moving out tomorrow."

"All right. Joseph, I do love you. I wouldn't be doing this if I didn't believe in our love."

"Let's not talk anymore," he said, placing his hand on her cheek. "I want to make love to you, Kendra. I want you so badly I ache."

Kendra turned her head to kiss the palm of Joseph's hand, tears misting her eyes.

"And I want you," she said softly. She wanted to be with him forever.

Joseph got to his feet and extended his hand to her. She placed hers in his, and together they went into the bedroom.

Nine

Joseph's residence was actually in Westland, a suburb near Detroit. It was a large, plushly furnished garden apartment with a spacious backyard for Homer. The way he wiggled his entire furry body, instead of just his nose, before Joseph let him outside, told Kendra that the rabbit was delighted to be there.

Kendra was not.

She was nervous and knew it, and was angry at herself at the realization. While she and Joseph had been in the apartment in Bay City the day before, she'd been filled with optimism about their future. They'd made sweet, slow, sensuous love over and over, before tackling once again the tedious chore of packing.

Kendra had wailed in dismay when Joseph had taken her snowball from the freezer and tossed it into the sink, but his promise that they would build her first snowman together had returned the smile to her lips. They laughed, talked and used every opportunity to move into each other's arms for a long kiss.

Again at night they had made love, kissing, touching, softly caressing, until passion burst into a bright, burning flame that threatened to consume them both. They'd come together urgently, almost roughly, to make their journey of ecstasy.

But during the long drive to Detroit, Kendra's euphoric mood had slowly dissipated. She had followed Joseph in her own car and had thought of the fragile state of their relationship. With the thoughts came the butterflies in her stomach and the nervous headache that pounded at her temples.

Joseph had given her a quick tour of his apartment, telling Kendra to take as much closet and drawer space as she needed. His housekeeper came in once a week to clean, he explained, but was still out of town. The woman adored Homer and took the rabbit home with her whenever Joseph had to be away.

"Well," Joseph said finally, "I'd better get to the office and see what's going on. In the meantime, you can get settled in. I'll stop by the hospital and see David while I'm out."

"Oh," Kendra said, frowning slightly, "all right. I'll unpack my things. Where should I put my boxes of odds and ends?"

"Like the baseball bat?" he asked, smiling at her. "Just stick them in the second bedroom for now. I'll see you later."

Joseph picked up his jacket and started for the door.

"Aren't you going to kiss me goodbye?"

"What? Oh, sure." He retraced his steps and brushed his lips over hers. "See you."

"Bye," Kendra murmured.

That man, she thought dismally, had nearly tripped over his feet to get away from her. He had assured her several times before they left Bay City that he totally agreed with her that they should live together in his apartment. Yet he seemed edgy, as if he didn't know quite what to do with her now that she was there.

Kendra sighed and went to unpack. The master bedroom was large, decorated in rich browns with splashes of orange. The king-size bed was covered by a spread in a diamond-shaped orange-and-brown pattern that matched the full-length drapes on the windows. The room had a masculine flair, but was warm and inviting.

Kendra unpacked, stacked her miscellaneous boxes in the corner of the guest room and lined her geraniums along the bar on the far wall of the living room. When she peered out the back door in search of Homer, the rabbit hopped away, busily exploring his own backyard.

"Okay, stay outside," Kendra said, shutting the door against the cold. "Desert me in my hour of need—I don't care."

She wandered around the spacious living room, telling herself this was her home now; this was where she would live with Joseph.

But she felt like a guest, a stranger, someone who had come to visit but didn't really belong. She would cook something, Kendra decided. She'd have a hot dinner on the table when Joseph returned.

As Kendra busied herself in the kitchen, she began to relax. She found a small beef roast in the freezer and defrosted it in the microwave. She surrounded it in a baking pan with potatoes, carrots and onions and put it in the oven. She made a crisp salad, then assembled ingredients for a cherry cobbler. Before long, delicious aromas began to waft through the air. She set the table, adding candles in ceramic holders, which she discovered in a bottom cupboard.

She had coordinated everything to be ready by six-thirty, telling herself that would allow Joseph time to end his workday and visit David in the hospital. She glanced at her watch and hurried into the bedroom.

Kendra ran warm water in the bathtub, stripped off her clothes and pinned her hair loosely on top of her head. With a sigh of pleasure, she sank into the soothing water, inhaling the lilac scent from the crystals she had added. Kendra could feel the tension ebb from her body as she leaned her head back against the tile wall and closed her eyes. Ten minutes later she reluctantly stepped out of the tub and dried herself with a fluffy towel, which she wrapped around her to survey the clothes in her section of the walk-in closet.

Nodding decisively, she slipped a pale lavender satin dressing gown over her lightly perfumed skin. She pulled the sash around her waist and viewed her reflection in the mirror. The gown hugged her breasts, then molded to her hips before draping to the floor. She brushed her hair, pushed her feet into white satin slippers and left the room.

Just as she entered the living room, Kendra heard the door open and stopped. Joseph entered; then to Kendra's wide-eyed horror a man, who looked enough like Joseph to be his twin, came in behind him.

"Hi," Joseph said, his gaze sweeping her from head to toe. "Kendra, this is Rick. Rick, this is Kendra."

"Hello," Rick said, smiling. "I feel I know you, Kendra. I hope you'll like living in Detroit. I understand you're going to be doing research for Joseph and David."

"Yeah, she is," Joseph said gruffly before Kendra could reply. "Kendra, why don't you get dressed?"

"Yes, of course," she said, spinning around. "I'll be right back. It's a pleasure meeting you, Rick," she added before hurrying from the room.

How embarrassing! she thought, feeling the warm flush on her cheeks as she closed the bedroom door. Well, how was she supposed to have known that Joseph would bring home one of his brothers?

She changed into jeans and a red-and-white striped sweater, plastered what she hoped was a calm, pleasant smile on her face and returned to the living room.

"Dinner is ready," she sang out. "There's plenty, Rick, if you'd care to join us."

"We had trays brought in and ate with David," Joseph told her.

"Thanks anyway, Kendra," Rick said. "I just stopped by to borrow Joseph's tennis racket. There's an indoor court at my health club, and I'm going to take on a doctor buddy of mine tomorrow morning."

"Good luck," Kendra said, managing a small smile. "Excuse me. I really must see to this food."

In the kitchen, Kendra yanked the roasting pan from the oven and plunked it none too gently onto the counter. She heard the low murmur of voices, then the closing of the door. Joseph appeared in the kitchen doorway and leaned his shoulder against the frame.

"Rick says I'm in trouble," he said.

"Oh?" she inquired, smacking the roast onto a platter. She picked up a spoon and flung the vegetables into a bowl with such force a potato catapulted back out, rolled across the counter and landed on the floor. Kendra ignored it.

"I didn't know you were going to cook dinner," Joseph said.

"I didn't know you were eating out," she replied, not looking at him.

"I'll be glad to eat again. Hospital food is really crummy. We were just keeping David company. That roast looks great. Smells great, too. Yeah, sure, I'll eat again, okay? Then maybe you could put that robe thing you were wearing back on. It was really something. Serve me a big plate of that stuff, Kendra, and I'll eat every bit. I—"

"Joseph," she said softly, turning to look at him.

"Yeah?"

"I love you."

"Come here," he said, holding out his arms to her.

Kendra ran across the room and into Joseph's embrace. He buried his face in the fragrant cloud of her hair.

"I'm sorry," he said. "Rick said I had sawdust for brains. I've been alone a long time, Kendra. I'm just not used to it mattering to anyone when I come and go. I'll get the hang of this. You'll see."

"I shouldn't have assumed you'd be ready to eat when you got here. I guess we have a lot to learn about living together."

"Yeah," he said quietly, "I guess we do. I just hope...
Well..."

"Hope what?" she asked, tilting her head back to look at him.

"That this is what you want. You thought you were meant to be a teacher but found out differently. So far, you've resented my protectiveness toward you. The way I see it, protecting and caring for you are part of my job, my role. I just wish I knew if this is where you really belong."

"Joseph, I know this is what I want. So much has happened that I realize you're having a difficult time believing that, but you'll come to see I mean it."

Joseph nodded, but there was a deep frown on his face.

"Would you like some cherry cobbler? I really don't expect you to eat another dinner."

"Cobbler sounds terrific," he said, then kissed her.

The kiss was deep and hard, and Kendra could feel the tension in Joseph's body. She responded instantly, molding against him, wanting to kiss away his doubts and the pain she had seen in his dark eyes. But as Joseph lifted his lips from hers, Kendra knew that a kiss wouldn't make it better. They needed time. They needed love.

While Kendra ate dinner and Joseph devoured two huge servings of cobbler, he told her that David would be released from the hospital in about two weeks. He would not, however, be able to return to work for several weeks after that.

"When David's a little stronger, I'll go over our caseload with him to see which ones we should try to farm out to other attorneys. We shouldn't have to trim back too drastically with you there to do the research."

"I'm eager to get started."

"Kendra, if you find that you really don't like doing law research, will you tell me?"

"Of course. I intend to be entirely honest with you about everything, all aspects of our lives."

"Good," he said gruffly. "That's fine. I'll take you to the law library tomorrow and let you see what you've let yourself in for. The place is grim."

The place, to Kendra, was marvelous.

Her eyes were shining as she roamed through the rows of thick volumes. Joseph showed her how to use the cross-indexed guide to locate pertinent cases. He gave her a hypothetical situation, and by following his instructions, Kendra proceeded to locate four similar cases.

"Man, you're smart," Joseph said. "I'm very impressed."

"When do I start for real? I can hardly wait."

Joseph chuckled. "Monday morning soon enough?"

"Oh, yes! This is so exciting. By the way, Mr. Bennett, as far as I can see, there isn't a speck of dust in here."

"Really?" he asked in mock surprise. "Guess they cleaned up the joint since I was here last."

"Guess so," she said, then kissed him soundly on the mouth. "You're devious, and I love you."

"Oh, yeah?" *Now* you love me. Wait until you spend a few days in here. You'll probably be ready to wring my neck. History, Kendra Smith, is boring."

"History, Joseph Bennett, is my second love after you."

"We'll see what tune you're singing Monday night."

And so it began.

On Monday morning Kendra followed Joseph to his office, where he introduced her to the secretary. He then reviewed with Kendra the case he was going to begin working on. Kendra carefully took notes, then drove to the law library. She took a deep breath as she entered the huge, quiet room.

At one o'clock she returned to Joseph's office to organize the information she discovered. Joseph was out of the office when she got there and hadn't returned by five o'clock, so Kendra drove home. When he arrived, at six, Kendra chattered on about her exhilarating day as she made dinner from the leftover roast. Joseph set the table but was very quiet through the entire meal.

"Joseph," Kendra said as they cleaned the kitchen, "is anything wrong?"

"No. I'm glad you enjoyed yourself today."

"Oh, I certainly did."

"Yeah, well, that digging into old news gets to you after awhile. I'll go feed Homer."

"Fine," she said absently, watching him leave the room. Oh, yes, she thought, there was something wrong with Joseph Bennett, all right. He was watching, waiting for her to voice her discontentment over her new job and then, no doubt, their relationship in general. He loved her, but he didn't really trust her to know her own mind. So be it. She would prove it to him. It would call for patience on her part. She loved him, and because she did, she would wait.

The days passed.

Kendra worked diligently at her task and produced detailed reports on the upcoming trial for Joseph's review. David was released from the hospital and sent home, where, his wife said, he was driving her straight out of her mind. Kendra met the Bennett clan and immediately liked them all. Mama Bennett was everything Joseph had said she was, and Kendra was enchanted by her. If Mrs. Bennett disapproved of Kendra and Joseph's living arrangements, she gave Kendra no clue of it. She did, however, glare often at Joseph and mutter things regarding praying for his soul. Kendra felt welcomed by the large family and looked forward to seeing them.

On the surface, everything seemed fine, but late at night after making love with Joseph, Kendra would lie awake. She would stare up into the darkness and face the fact that Joseph's underlying tension had not diminished. She would glance up in the evening to find him studying her, looking at her as though he were seeking the path to her soul.

One night, after Kendra had been in Detroit for three weeks, she once again found herself unable to sleep. Joseph was breathing steadily next to her. She left the bed, doing her best not to wake him, pulled on her robe and went into the kitchen, where she prepared a mug of hot chocolate. With a sigh she sat down at the table, cradling the mug between her hands.

No tomorrows, she thought suddenly. That's what was missing from her life with Joseph. They never spoke of the future. They worked exceptionally well together on a professional level, and Joseph was quick to praise her exacting reports. They shared the household chores while waiting for the housekeeper to return, and had a busy schedule of enjoyable social activities.

But they had no tomorrows, no plans, no dreams they whispered of while snuggled close together. And, inch by emotional inch, Kendra's resolve to wait patiently for Joseph to believe in her was crumbling. His unspoken distrust was beginning to hurt.

At family gatherings, Kendra realized, Joseph skillfully avoided addressing any subjects pertaining to the future. When one of his sisters spoke of a new summer vacation spot that had opened in upper Michigan, Joseph had shrugged and said that summer was a long way off.

During Thanksgiving dinner, Mama Bennett had clucked her tongue and said it was a shame there was no Bennett baby in the high chair that year. Joseph had asked to have the potatoes passed to him.

Oh, Joseph, Kendra sighed, how long would it be before they had their tomorrows? There was such a void in their lives with no hopes and dreams.

"What are you doing out here?" Joseph asked, appearing in the kitchen doorway. He'd tugged on his jeans, and he looked rumpled and sleepy.

"Having some hot chocolate. Would you like some?"

"No. Couldn't you sleep?"

"No."

"Why not?" he asked, sitting in the chair opposite her. "It's nearly one. What's wrong? Don't you feel well?"

"I feel fine. Sort of."

"Meaning?"

"Oh, Joseph," she said, sighing, "I feel as though we're living in limbo or some kind of twilight zone. Except for discussing your cases, we don't talk about tomorrow until it becomes today. I can really relate to people who are on trial. Their fate rests in a jury's hands. My future rests in yours. I don't know what else to do to prove to you how much I love you. When, Joseph? When are we going to have some tomorrows?''

"What do you want from me?" he demanded, his jaw tightening. "A date circled in red on the calendar, a date when all my doubts and fears are guaranteed to have vanished?"

"No, of course not, but—"

"Yeah, okay, you really seem to have found your place doing the research. And I've never questioned that you love me."

"Nor," Kendra said, leaning toward him, "have I voiced any objection to calling you to tell you I've arrived safely at the law library. I let Rick give me a flu shot at your insistence and agreed to buy a heavier coat. I didn't fake my acceptance of your directives; I've viewed them as lovely examples of your caring. What else, Joseph? What else can I do? I want to marry you. I want our baby to be in the Bennett high chair next Thanksgiving. Next Thanksgiving? You won't even commit yourself to making plans with me for next week!"

"Don't push it, Kendra."

"Yes, Joseph," she said tremulously, "I *am* going to push it. We're not living; we're existing in a shallow world. The depth in a relationship comes not only from love but from mutual goals, dreams, hopes, plans for the future. We have no solid foundation. We could shatter into a million pieces and wonder what happened. Please, Joseph, give us a chance. Give us the tomorrows we deserve. I'm asking you to marry me.''

Emotions played across Joseph's face as Kendra watched him, her heartbeat thundering in her ears. She saw his anger, then a frown that spoke of confusion, then a shadow of pain. Seconds passed, and still he didn't speak.

"No," he said finally, his voice flat and low.

"I can't live this way, Joseph," she whispered, tears filling her eyes. "It's too empty, too cold, without tomorrows."

Joseph stared at her for a long moment, then slowly got to his feet as though the effort required his last ounce of energy. Without speaking, he turned and walked from the room.

Kendra didn't move. She just sat there, tears streaming down her face as she clutched her mug so tightly her knuckles turned white. A few minutes later she heard the front door close.

Joseph was gone.

Kendra covered her face with her hands and wept.

It wasn't until the first gray streaks of the winter dawn crept below the curtains on the window that she stumbled to her feet and went into the bedroom. With trembling hands she lifted the telephone receiver and called Matt. Kendra poured out her story, not bothering to brush the fresh tears from her cheeks.

"I'm telling you this not because you're a priest but because you're Joseph's brother. I have to know he'll be all right," Kendra said, "that you won't allow him to start working too hard again."

"Kendra, running away never solved anything."

"I'm not making Joseph happy, Matt. He wants a wife and family but doesn't believe in me enough to allow us to go forward. When Joseph met me, I was floundering, trying to discover who I was, where I belonged. I made mistakes, had to start over. But Joseph doesn't trust me enough to know that I want to be with him always. I've got to leave. It's the kindest thing I can do for him. Watch over him for me, Matt. I love him so much."

"Of course I will. Right after I bust his jaw."

"Priests aren't supposed to punch people," Kendra said, managing a smile.

"That was spoken as a brother. That Joseph is so stubborn it's a sin. Where are you going?"

"I think I'll go back to Port Payne until I decide what to do. I really did enjoy working in the law library. Perhaps I'll check out jobs similar to that, but not in Detroit. There're too many memories here."

"I'm so sorry about this, Kendra."

"Thank you, Matt. All you Bennetts have been wonderful."

"Except Joseph. He's a louse."

"No, he's a man with a lot of pride. I'll always love him. Goodbye, Matt."

"God bless you, Kendra Smith."

Kendra showered, dressed, then packed only one suitcase. She didn't have the energy to load all her belongings once again into her car. None of the things she owned seemed important. Nothing seemed to matter. She kept her tears at bay as she watered the geraniums for the last time, but sobbed uncontrollably as she hugged Homer goodbye. As though sensing her distress, he nuzzled her cheek with his nose.

"Bye, Homer," she said tearfully. "Take care of Joseph for me."

She set the rabbit on the floor, placed one geranium in front of him as a parting gift, then picked up her suitcase and left the apartment.

Kendra knew tongues were wagging in Port Payne when she returned and rented her cabin again, but she didn't particularly care what speculations anyone was making about her. She just wanted to be left alone.

She got her wish. A heavy snow fell that night, making it impossible for Kendra to budge much past her front porch. She spent the next three days reliving her memories of Joseph, crying for Joseph, smiling gently at various scenarios in her mind, all involving Joseph.

On the morning of the fourth day, Kendra was awakened by the sound of a heavy, chugging motor. She pulled on her robe, stuffed her feet into her slippers and went into the living room to peer through the front curtains.

"A snowplow," she mumbled. "A snowplow? My, Port Payne is coming up in the world."

To Kendra's amazement, a man jumped off the machine and sprinted to her cabin. Kendra opened the door a crack.

"Yes?" she said.

"Kendra Smith?"

"Yes."

"Delivery, ma'am. Wait now, I have to do this right." He pulled two small brown bags from his coat pocket. "Yeah, okay. You open the square one first, then the round one. Have a good day, ma'am."

"But..." she said as he shoved the bags at her. "Who..."

"Square, then round," he yelled over his shoulder as he ran back to the snowplow.

Kendra closed the door and stared at the two bags.

"Well, only one way to find out, I guess," she said, moving to sit on the sofa.

The square package contained a box of tea.

The round object was an orange.

There was no card in either bag.

"Weird," she said. "Very weird."

By the middle of the morning, Kendra had looked at the strange gifts so often she decided she was close to losing her sanity. Since the road was now clear she drove to Port Payne and parked in front of the grocery store.

"Yoo-hoo, Kendra," Mrs. Howell called from the post-office doorway. "I have something for you, dear."

"Coming," Kendra said.

Mrs. Howell produced two brown bags. Kendra looked at her disbelievingly.

"Mrs. Howell, who told you to give these to me?" Kendra asked.

"Oh, it was... Land's sake, I can't remember. Memory isn't what it used to be, you know. I do remember you're supposed to open the squishy one first, then the round one."

"Squishy?"

"Squishy," Mrs. Howell repeated, nodding decisively.

"Right," Kendra said, peering into the bag.

"What is it, dear?"

"A bag of marshmallows." Kendra opened the other bag. "And another orange. This is crazy."

"Gifts are gifts, Kendra," Mrs. Howell said sternly. "Oh, would you take this mail to the McCauley sisters at the drugstore?"

"What? Oh, certainly. Are you positive you don't remember who—"

"My mind is a blank."

"Mmm," Kendra said, leaving the post office with the marshmallows and orange.

The fact that the McCauley twins each held a brown bag when Kendra arrived at the drugstore somehow simply did not surprise her.

"So tell me," Kendra began, folding her arms over her breasts, "which one do I open first?"

"Oh, it really doesn't matter," said one of the twins.

"I see. Any chance you remember who asked you to give these to me?"

"Not a chance in a million," the other twin said, smiling sweetly. "You're dealing with very old gray matter here, Kendra," she added, tapping her temple with her fingertip.

Kendra glared at them before opening the bags. "Oh," she gasped. "How lovely."

"A rose," a twin said. "And another rose. Oh, aren't they pretty? Kendra, dear, would you stop by the grocery and tell Fred Frazier his cough medicine came in?"

"I wouldn't miss it for the world." Kendra scooped up her treasures and stomped out of the store.

Mrs. Willoby hailed Kendra before she'd gone twenty feet. The brown bag she handed Kendra contained another orange.

"The whole town has flipped out," Kendra muttered as she entered the grocery store. "Okay, Mr. Frazier, give me the brown bag, then tell me how forgetful you are."

"Here you go," he said, beaming as he gave her the bag.

It contained a plastic windmill.

"How cute," Kendra said dryly. "Am I finished yet? May I go home now?"

"Not quite. Libby wants to see you at her stained-glass store."

"Okeydokey. Then I'll have myself committed."

Mr. Frazier's laughter followed Kendra out the door. She juggled the various items in her arms as she walked along.

It was some sort of game, a puzzle, Kendra mused. The people of Port Payne were not idiots. They knew that her sudden return without Joseph meant that there was trouble between the lovers. They'd obviously concocted a diversion that they hoped would cheer her up.

How sweet they all are, Kendra thought. Well, she should be grateful, be a good sport. Okay, the gifts had to mean something, and the order she had received them in had been important. Tea. Then an orange. Then marshmallows and another orange. Two roses, an orange and a windmill. "That makes no sense," she murmured. And now she was headed for Libby's store. "I don't get it."

Unless... Kendra pondered. Unless...

She stopped in her tracks.

Tea for *T*, she thought, her heart beginning to race. Orange for *O*. Marshmallows for *M*. *O* for orange, two *R*s for the roses. Another *O* for orange. A *W* for the windmill. And now she was going to Libby's stained-glass store. *S*. It spelled TOMORROWS!

"Joseph?" she whispered. "Joseph!" she yelled, then took off at a run.

Joseph stepped out of Libby's store just as Kendra came flying along the sidewalk.

"Joseph!"

"Ah, Kendra," he moaned, and held out his arms to her.

She flung herself at him to be caught by his strong arms as oranges and roses and all the other treasures tumbled to the ground. Joseph's mouth melted over Kendra's in a kiss that was long and powerful and brought tears to Kendra's eyes.

"Kendra," Joseph said when he lifted his head, "forgive me for being so stubborn. Forgive me for not believing in you. I was filled with fear, numbed by it. I'd been alone so long, and then there you were. I was in love for the first time in my life. There were so many changes so quickly and... Kendra, I couldn't think about our tomorrows because I was so afraid I was going to lose you."

"Oh, Joseph."

"I couldn't handle it, thinking about facing those tomorrows without you. I just wanted to live in the right now because you were still with me."

"Joseph, I love you. I'll never leave you."

"I know that now. I went over it all again in my mind, Kendra, and this time I listened—really listened—to what you said. Everything we had together was so good, so real. All you were asking of me, of my love, was to believe in you, and grant us the chance of having our tomorrows. Will you share them with me? Will you marry me, Kendra Smith?"

"Yes. Oh, yes, Joseph," she said, tears spilling onto her cheeks.

Joseph gave her a quick, hard kiss, then raised one fist straight up in the air. The signal was received, and the doors to all the stores were flung open, the citizens of Port Payne spilling out onto the sidewalk.

"We did it," Libby said, smiling. "What a team we have in Port Payne. Be happy, both of you. Oh, and Homer, too."

"Thank you, Libby," Kendra said, smiling through her tears.

"Thanks, everybody," Joseph yelled.

A round of applause went up from the spectators.

"Let's go home, Kendra," Joseph said, pulling her against him. "There're a slew of Bennetts in Detroit who aren't speaking to me and who will be very glad to see you. Besides, there's an empty-high-chair project we should start working on. I love you."

"And I love you, Joseph," she said, nestling closer to his side. "I love you, and Homer. I love all the Bennetts. And, oh, how I love my wonderful new shoes."

*   *   *   *   *

*. . . and now an exciting short story
from Silhouette Books.*

*

HEATHER GRAHAM POZZESSERE

Shadows on the Nile

CHAPTER ONE

Alex could tell that the woman was very nervous. Her
fingers were wound tightly about the arm rests, and she
had been staring straight ahead since the flight began.
Who was she? Why was she flying alone? Why to
Egypt? She was a small woman, fine-boned, with clas-
sical features and porcelain skin. Her hair was golden
blond, and she had blue-gray eyes that were slightly
tilted at the corners, giving her a sensual and exotic appeal.

And she smelled divine. He had been sitting there,
glancing through the flight magazine, and her scent had
reached him, filling him like something rushing through
his bloodstream, and before he had looked at her he had
known that she would be beautiful.

John was frowning at him. His gaze clearly said that
this was not the time for Alex to become interested in a
woman. Alex lowered his head, grinning. Nuts to John.
He was the one who had made the reservations so late
that there was already another passenger between them
in their row. Alex couldn't have remained silent anyway; he was certain that he could ease the flight for her.

Besides, he had to know her name, had to see if her eyes would turn silver when she smiled. Even though he should, he couldn't ignore her.

"Alex," John said warningly.

Maybe John was wrong, Alex thought. Maybe this was precisely the right time for him to get involved. A woman would be the perfect shield, in case anyone was interested in his business in Cairo.

The two men should have been sitting next to each other, Jillian decided. She didn't know why she had wound up sandwiched between the two of them, but she couldn't do a thing about it. Frankly, she was far too nervous to do much of anything.

"It's really not so bad," a voice said sympathetically. It came from her right. It was the younger of the two men, the one next to the window. "How about a drink? That might help."

Jillian took a deep, steadying breath, then managed to answer. "Yes . . . please. Thank you."

His fingers curled over hers. Long, very strong fingers, nicely tanned. She had noticed him when she had taken her seat—he was difficult not to notice. There was an arresting quality about him. He had a certain look: high-powered, confident, self-reliant. He was medium tall and medium built, with shoulders that nicely filled out his suit jacket, dark brown eyes, and sandy hair that seemed to defy any effort at combing it. And he had a wonderful voice, deep and compelling. It broke through her fear and actually soothed her. Or perhaps it was the warmth of his hand over hers that did it.

"Your first trip to Egypt?" he asked. She managed a brief nod, but was saved from having to comment when the stewardess came by. Her companion ordered her a white wine, then began to converse with her quite normally, as if unaware that her fear of flying had nearly rendered her speechless. He asked her what she did for a living, and she heard herself tell him that she was a music teacher at a junior college. He responded easily to everything she said, his voice warm and concerned each time he asked another question. She didn't think; she simply answered him, because flying had become easier the moment he touched her. She even told him that she was a widow, that her husband had been killed in a car accident four years ago, and that she was here now to fulfill a long-held dream, because she had always longed to see the pyramids, the Nile and all the ancient wonders Egypt held.

She had loved her husband, Alex thought, watching as pain briefly darkened her eyes. Her voice held a thread of sadness when she mentioned her husband's name. Out of nowhere, he wondered how it would feel to be loved by such a woman.

Alex noticed that even John was listening, commenting on things now and then. How interesting, Alex thought, looking across at his friend and associate.

The stewardess came with the wine. Alex took it for her, chatting casually with the woman as he paid. Charmer, Jillian thought ruefully. She flushed, realizing that it was his charm that had led her to tell him so much about her life.

Her fingers trembled when she took the wineglass. "I'm sorry," she murmured. "I don't really like to fly."

Alex—he had introduced himself as Alex, but without telling her his last name—laughed and said that was the understatement of the year. He pointed out the window to the clear blue sky—an omen of good things to come, he said—then assured her that the airline had an excellent safety record. His friend, the older man with the haggard, world-weary face, eventually introduced himself as John. He joked and tried to reassure her, too, and eventually their efforts paid off. Once she felt a little calmer, she offered to move, so they could converse without her in the way.

Alex tightened his fingers around hers, and she felt the startling warmth in his eyes. His gaze was appreciative and sensual, without being insulting. She felt a rush of sweet heat swirl within her, and she realized with surprise that it was excitement, that she was enjoying his company the way a woman enjoyed the company of a man who attracted her. She had thought she would never feel that way again.

"I wouldn't move for all the gold in ancient Egypt," he said with a grin, "and I doubt that John would, either." He touched her cheek. "I might lose track of you, and I don't even know your name."

"Jillian," she said, meeting his eyes. "Jillian Jacoby."

He repeated her name softly, as if to commit it to memory, then went on to talk about Cairo, the pyramids at Giza, the Valley of the Kings, and the beauty of the nights when the sun set over the desert in a riot of blazing red.

And then the plane was landing. To her amazement, the flight had ended. Once she was on solid ground again, Jillian realized that Alex knew all sorts of things about her, while she didn't know a thing about him or John—not even their full names.

They went through customs together. Jillian was immediately fascinated, in love with the colorful atmosphere of Cairo, and not at all dismayed by the waiting and the bureaucracy. When they finally reached the street she fell head over heels in love with the exotic land. The heat shimmered in the air, and taxi drivers in long burnooses lined up for fares. She could hear the soft singsong of their language, and she was thrilled to realize that the dream she had harbored for so long was finally coming true.

She didn't realize that two men had followed them from the airport to the street. Alex, however, did. He saw the men behind him, and his jaw tightened as he nodded to John to stay put and hurried after Jillian.

"Where are you staying?" he asked her.

"The Hilton," she told him, pleased at his interest. Maybe her dream was going to turn out to have some unexpected aspects.

He whistled for a taxi. Then, as the driver opened the door, Jillian looked up to find Alex staring at her. She felt...something. A fleeting magic raced along her spine, as if she knew what he was about to do. Knew, and should have protested, but couldn't.

Alex slipped his arm around her. One hand fell to her waist, the other cupped her nape, and he kissed her. His mouth was hot, his touch firm, persuasive. She was filled with heat; she trembled...and then she broke away at last, staring at him, the look in her eyes more eloquent than any words. Confused, she turned away and stepped into the taxi. As soon as she was seated she turned to stare after him, but he was already gone, a part of the crowd.

She touched her lips as the taxi sped toward the heart of the city. She shouldn't have allowed the kiss; she barely knew him. But she couldn't forget him.

She was still thinking about him when she reached the Hilton. She checked in quickly, but she was too late to acquire a guide for the day. The manager suggested that she stop by the Kahil bazaar, not far from the hotel. She dropped her bags in her room, then took another taxi to the bazaar. Once again she was enchanted. She loved everything: the noise, the people, the donkey carts that blocked the narrow streets, the shops with their beaded entryways and beautiful wares in silver and stone, copper and brass. Old men smoking water pipes sat on mats drinking tea, while younger men shouted out their wares from stalls and doorways. Jillian began walking slowly, trying to take it all in. She was occasionally jostled, but she kept her hand on her purse and sidestepped quickly. She was just congratulating herself on her competence when she was suddenly dragged into an alley by two Arabs swaddled in burnooses.

"What—" she gasped, but then her voice suddenly fled. The alley was empty and shadowed, and night was coming. One man had a scar on his cheek, and held a long, curved knife; the other carried a switchblade.

"Where is it?" the first demanded.

"Where is what?" she asked frantically.

The one with the scar compressed his lips grimly. He set his knife against her cheek, then stroked the flat side down to her throat. She could feel the deadly coolness of the steel blade.

"Where is it? Tell me now!"

Her knees were trembling, and she tried to find the breath to speak. Suddenly she noticed a shadow emerging from the darkness behind her attackers. She gasped, stunned, as the man drew nearer. It was Alex.

Alex...silent, stealthy, his features taut and grim. Her heart seemed to stop. Had he come to her rescue? Or was he allied with her attackers, there to threaten, even destroy, her?

* * * * *

Watch for Chapter Two of SHADOWS ON THE NILE coming next month—only in Silhouette Intimate Moments.

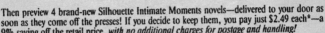
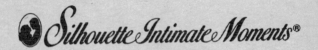

ATTRACTIVE, SPACE SAVING BOOK RACK

Display your most prized novels on this handsome and sturdy book rack. The hand-rubbed walnut finish will blend into your library decor with quiet elegance, providing a practical organizer for your favorite hard-or soft-covered books.

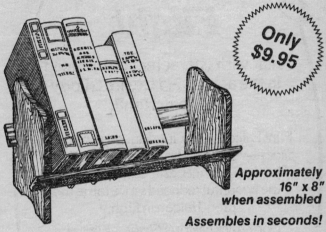

Only $9.95

Approximately 16" x 8" when assembled

Assembles in seconds!

To order, rush your name, address and zip code, along with a check or money order for $10.70* ($9.95 plus 75¢ postage and handling) payable to *Silhouette Books.*

Silhouette Books
Book Rack Offer
901 Fuhrmann Blvd.
P.O. Box 1396
Buffalo, NY 14269-1396

Offer not available in Canada.

*New York and Iowa residents add appropriate sales tax.

BKR-2A

 **Silhouette Desire**

COMING NEXT MONTH

#385 LADY BE GOOD—Jennifer Greene
To Clay, Liz was a lady in the true sense of the word, but she wanted more from him than adoration from afar—she wanted him to be this particular lady's man.

#386 PURE CHEMISTRY—Naomi Horton
Chemist Jill Benedict had no intention of ever seeing newsman Hunter Kincaid again. Hunter was bent on tracking her down and convincing her that they were an explosive combination.

#387 IN YOUR WILDEST DREAMS—Mary Alice Kirk
Caroline Forrester met Greg Lawton over an argument about a high school sex ed course. It didn't take long for them to learn that they had a thing or two to teach each other—about love!

#388 DOUBLE SOLITAIRE—Sara Chance
One look at Leigh Mason told Joshua Dancer that she was the woman for him. She might have been stubbornly nursing a broken heart, but Josh knew he'd win her love—hands down.

#389 A PRINCE OF A GUY—Kathleen Korbel
Down-to-earth Casey Phillips was a dead ringer for Princess Cassandra of Moritania. Dashing Prince Eric von Lieberhaven convinced her to impersonate the kidnapped heiress to the throne, but could she convince him he was her king of hearts?

#390 FALCON'S FLIGHT—Joan Hohl
Both Leslie Fairfield and Flint Falcon were gamblers at heart—but together they found that the stakes were higher than either had expected when the payoff was love. Featuring characters you've met in Joan Hohl's acclaimed trilogy for Desire.

In response
to last year's outstanding success,
Silhouette Brings You:

Silhouette Christmas Stories 1987

Specially chosen for you in a delightful volume celebrating the holiday season, four original romantic stories written by four of your favorite Silhouette authors.

Dixie Browning—*Henry the Ninth*
Ginna Gray—*Season of Miracles*
Linda Howard—*Bluebird Winter*
Diana Palmer—*The Humbug Man*

Each of these bestselling authors will enchant you with their unforgettable stories, exuding the magic of Christmas and the wonder of falling in love.

A heartwarming Christmas gift during the holiday season... indulge yourself and give this book to a special friend!

Available November 1987

XM87-1